PHOENIX RISING

By

CARA CARNES

ca

Decadent Publishing Company
www.decadentpublishing.com

Phoenix Rising
Copyright © 2014 by Cara Carnes
ISBN: 978-1-61333-755-4
Cover art by Syneca Featherstone

Published by Decadent Publishing Company, LLC
Look for us online at:
www.decadentpublishing.com

ROAR

Mischief, Mongrels & Mayhem
Sorority Wolf by Rebecca Royce
Imperfect Mate by Lia Davis
Shifted Plans by Brandy Walker
Tempting her Tiger by Virginia Cavanaugh

Dear Reader,

Welcome to autumn, 2014. It's a time for pumpkin spice lattes, cooling days, and kids heading back to school. I swear it feels like just yesterday that we were doing this last year. You know, I have a deep and abiding love for paranormal romance. I actually fell in love with urban fantasy and by extension paranormals thanks to two authors: Anne Rice and Emma Bull. If you've never checked them out, you should.

Fortunately, in the years since I read those the genre of paranormal romance has grown by leaps, shifts, fangs, and fur. I've always had a soft spot for shifter romance, and if you told me a book had wolves or cats or bears in it—well, I was so there. This hasn't changed, not one bit. I don't think there's enough shifter romance in the world, but I did want to see more—what happens when young shifters leave their packs? What if they go off to school? How do they start over? How does a young wolf or cat or bear or any young person really make that final leap to adulthood?

I am thrilled to introduce Decadent ROAR as an answer to those questions. The line is dedicated to featuring stories about young weres and shifters who have come of age but now must determine the path of the rest of their lives. It's an exciting time of making your own decisions and not having to seek permission, but freedom always comes with a cost. Fortunately for these burgeoning adults, they have the ROAR hotline to reach out to.

Run by the mysterious siblings Hui and Min, 555-ROAR is a line shifters can text or call for help, whether it's, *What's the best spot to hunt*, or *I'm in danger. What should I do*? It's a helpline, and a lifeline in some cases. Growing up is hard—being an adult is harder.

So what do we have to kick you off as ROAR launches a new school year? How about a mongrel attending college close to home who must contend with a sexy Alpha and his pride moving into her region? That's the problem Mischief "Missy" Jones faces in **Mischief, Mongrels & Mayhem** by Heather Long.

Pledging a sorority can be hell, but is it so bad when you have a demon on your side? Werewolf Alexandra will have to decide when Kieran promises to turn over heaven and hell to help her out in **Sorority Wolf** by Rebecca Royce.

Not everyone gets encouragement when they head off into the big, bad world on their own. This couldn't be more true for fragile and abused Riletta who's dumped at school with no options, no fallback, and no hope—that is until delicious Macen intervenes in the hot ride that is **Phoenix Rising** by Cara Carnes.

Choosing college can be a grueling experience, but, then again, so can diving into adulthood and taking responsibility for your actions. Samira faces s a lot of hard choices, none tougher than accepting human Gavin might be her mate in Lia Davis' **Imperfect Mates.**

Life is what happens when you're not paying attention, and the best things don't always occur in the order you expect. They sure don't for Avery and Declan.

Both are busy setting up their lives but the allure of mating throws them for a loop in Brandy Walker's **Shifted Plans.**

Attracting attention from the male species is a hard job, even more so when that male is a shifter. Some lines, though, are hard to cross, and Jordan will fight his attraction to his best friend's sister, Stacia, with everything he has in **Tempting her Tiger** by Virginia Cavanaugh.

Ultimately, the question these six stories must answer is not who will they be as adults, but who are they? How do they reconcile everything they've ever known with what can be? It's a new type of shifter romance, with all the love and passion required to achieve a happily ever after....

Thank you for joining us as we launch a hot new series—we'll do our best to make every single tale memorable.

Happy Reading!
Heather Long and
Decadent Publishing
www.decadentpublishing.com

~Dedication~

Decadent Publishing for all their hard work and to the fabulous Rebecca Royce for encouraging me to write this book. I'm thankful every day for your friendship.

Chapter One

Riletta

"Don't make a scene, Riletta. Get out, and do not speak."

Unease pricked my skin. I fumbled with the door latch for a moment before it gave way, and I tumbled out of the black BMW. A crisp breeze ripped through the rustling trees around us. I would've grabbed my jacket had I known we were going somewhere.

I stretched the soreness from my body as Jacob Cervantez slammed the trunk and set a suitcase on the ground before me. My gaze darted around, my brain disoriented from the shock and the utter silence that had been my only companion the past several hours.

"This is the only university willing to accept you due to your limitations. I doubt you're worth the favors I had to call in, but the pack will benefit from this sacrifice. At least we'll be relieved of the burden your presence created." The gruff tone made me step backward until I pressed against the car door I'd shut at some point. "Registration ends in an hour. I suggest you get in before they change their mind."

Registration? My mouth opened and then shut as I processed what to ask first if given the chance. I'd learned years ago to choose my words wisely because I rarely got the answers I expected.

"I didn't know—"

"Riletta. Did I say you could speak?"

I cast my gaze downward and shrank into myself.

"You're lucky I don't have time to teach you etiquette. You aren't my problem anymore."

What did that mean? He shoved his hand into his pocket with an exasperated sigh and grabbed a few hundreds off the massive wad of cash he always carried. The Alpha of the Cervantez pack would never be caught without funds. "Elise is too soft-hearted. She insisted you be given something until you get settled."

Settled. He was dumping me here. My heart sped; my breath quickened. Equal parts of fear and hope fought for my attention.

"Don't think I'll allow her to give you more, so make it last. It'll probably take a few months for them to handle your paperwork. They'll have problems securing you since no one knows *what the hell you are*."

Amusement glimmered in his gaze when I cringed at the insult. I took the wad of cash and shoved it into my jean pocket. "Thanks."

"You'd better listen up, Riletta." Pain erupted along my bruised arm when he grabbed me and shook hard until my teeth rattled and my head pounded. "They'll ask for your designation when you enter. Under no circumstances are you to reference my pack. I allowed your existence, but that doesn't mean I accept responsibility. Nod if you understand, Riletta."

I nodded and shrank away from his menacing presence when he leaned forward. Garlic and alcohol burned my nostrils. The stench was nauseating, but made me recall the hunger I'd been trying to ignore. Swallowing, I pressed on my stomach, willing the rumble to subside. How long had it been since I'd eaten? One, two days?

"That's what you get for being too uppity to eat pizza."

You know I love pizza, you miserable prick. That's why you piled it with meat I was allergic to. Every meal he oversaw in the pack focused on meat. The anger vibrated within me until my body trembled with a need to react. Just this once.

"Go. I've wasted enough time dealing with you." He prowled to his door and paused to glare over the vehicle. "Keep your trap shut about my pack and your presence there, or you'll be sorry."

I nodded mutely, palmed the handle of my suitcase, and dragged it across the parking lot. The massive structure before me appeared to be some form of gymnasium or large meeting facility since there were no windows. I kept my gaze downward and ignored the jostling of the other bodies slamming into me from both sides. Surely the lone door offered refuge, a quiet place to breathe and absorb what had just happened.

You're almost there. Don't panic.

He threw me out of the pack.

Knowing something was inevitable and accepting its occurrence were two entirely different things. Part of me wanted to race after the long-gone car or perhaps call Elise and beg to return. But that was crazy. They'd been done with me eighteen years, three months and two days ago—the moment I'd crawled into their land from no one knew where. I'd been two when they'd proclaimed me a freak of nature undeserving of life.

But I'd been spared.

Piercing shrieks and laughter drew my focus from my trudge forward to a crush of girls several yards away. I smiled cautiously when a few of them met my stare. Fitting in had never been my strong suit, but perhaps this place was different.

Pain streamed through my core, radiating from my face when I slammed into an unmoving object—a massive chest adorned in a crimson T-shirt with a black-and-white snapping wolf. My throat constricted for a moment as I studied the muscular flesh beneath the shirt. He was huge.

"Slow your roll there, mouse." Warm fingers wrapped gently around both my arms, holding me up for a moment as my limbs forgot how to work. His full lips turned upward into a smug grin before he shoved me backward. My pulse slammed into overdrive as I met a metallic gray gaze. A rugged jaw line drew attention from his gorgeous face to the wavy mass of thick, black hair, longer than fashionable, which flirted with his shirt collar.

This was someone who realized the effect he had on girls like me. I studied his shirt for a moment, reining in my riotous body. My lungs burned for breaths I couldn't remember to take; something within me rubbed against my skin.

The sensation made me gasp. *What the hell was that?* Could it be…?

No. There was no way. I'd been tested. Repeatedly.

I was inherently damaged beyond repair.

Defective.

"Breathe, little mouse. Nice and deep for me."

Fingers squeezed until I inhaled the welcoming brush of woodsy brine and earth deep into my lungs. I wanted to lean into his warmth, inhale deeper at his pulse point like I'd seen others from my pack do with the Alphas. He was utterly splendid in all ways.

I knew better than to surrender to the desire, though.

Abominations like you will not breathe the same air as my Alphas, Riletta. Don't offend them with your presence. You exist because I showed mercy. Don't make me regret my decision.

"Sorry." The squeak of my rarely-used voice made me shrivel away from the strength of his embrace. Could I be any more pathetic?

I hardened my stance and waited for the slap, the shove. I'd been foolish to not notice him within my field of vision. I'd dared to slam into an Alpha. I closed my eyes, cringed, and waited.

And waited. Chancing a peek at the gorgeous man before me, my heart flailed for normalcy, beating wildly until my brain could process his reaction. He grinned.

No one ever grinned when I spoke, when they sensed what I wasn't. I'd met his kind before. "If you'll please excuse me, I need to register before they close."

"Of course." He maneuvered to the side and opened the door.

I forced a smile of gratitude and stepped into the massive room, which echoed with the hum of conversations and revelry. Hundreds, possibly thousands, of people filled the large building. The swirling crowd created a noxious, heated cloud of sweat and perfumed stench. I covered my nose and breathed through my mouth.

I can't do this.

Nervousness froze me. I knew nothing. This place wasn't for me.

Emotion choked me, and I forced back the fear welling in my eyes. I'd dreamed of my release from Jacob's control for years, plotting and planning what I'd do. I'd never fathomed this as my fate. How stupid was I?

Jacob always, always chose the worst scenario for me. This was my living nightmare—all those people. Humans—whom I'd never been around—and shifters—who'd declared me an abomination.

I'd become too complacent. This was my punishment for being ill-prepared.

Realizing the massive wolf I'd slammed into still loomed beside me, I inhaled deeply through my mouth and ordered myself to move. Avoidance only created more trouble. *Accept your fate, and move the hell on.* It'd been my motto for years and saved me many nights.

"Thanks." The dismissal seemed to go unheard as he dragged me forward. God, he was tall. Taller than Jacob—and not many could say that since the Alpha leader was well over six foot. This guy was much wider across the chest, too, but his hips were lean, his legs long and powerful thighs beneath his jeans. "I can handle it from here."

"This way."

He tunneled a path through the crowd with his muscular body, my suitcase in tow. When had he gotten my suitcase?

I followed helplessly, darting apologetic gazes to unseen masses of people as I hurried along in his wake until we entered a smaller second room. I took a few moments to look around, relieved we'd parted company with the crush of bodies in the other room. Folding tables, manned by a couple of people at each, formed a half-moon in the room.

A few students stood at most of them, chatting away with the smiling attendants. Human. Fae. Wolves. Lions. Tigers. Pumas. I read shifter faction after shifter faction, each one slicing my soul. Each beautifully decorated sign, complete with colorful emblems, sealed me within a tomb of doubt. The encroaching apprehension squeezed, crushing my few moments of normalcy with brutal efficiency.

I was none of those things.

"Well?" He flashed a grin and crossed his arms. "Don't leave me guessing all day, sweet mouse."

Heat streamed through me. I grabbed the suitcase beside him before he could stop me and studied the options one final time. A handwritten piece of poster board leaning against the wall denoted my fate.

Other.

I foraged what self-confidence I'd squirreled away and closed the distance between me and the desolate table. I could feel the stares of those around me as I nudged my way past the lingering wolves and tigers.

Several shouted to the looming shadow I'd inherited. *"Macen."*

The name continued echoing around me in a stream of welcomes, which agitated me. Maybe he wasn't following me. He'd done his obligatory duty and gotten me in here—wherever "here" was. I thought a moment before I took the final few steps to the table.

The coastal scent of pine and salt water had rippled through Macen's aura when I'd been near enough to scent him. The memory heated my insides with a renewed awareness of the man still shadowing me, even though we'd passed his pack moments ago. The unique musk already embedded in my brain as *him* blanketed me in the realization I was not alone—he was there behind me, his heat near enough for me to sense, yet distant enough for me not to flinch in discomfort. Why was he still there? Did he mean his presence to be comforting or threatening?

I'd grown accustomed to being the bug under the proverbial microscope of existence. Pinned in place and unwillingly sliced apart time and again by others for amusement or perhaps to appease curiosity, I'd numbed to the ridicule and animosity.

Until now.

Whispers traveled as I closed the distance between me and the scowling blonde with large, barely contained breasts jutting out from an obviously modified Wolf Pack shirt. She scowled and leaned toward me, thrusting her tits forward—no doubt for Macen's benefit and not mine. Grabbing a pencil and the sole sheet of paper in front of her, she sliced a blue-eyed stare my direction.

"Well? Who are you?"

"Riletta." Cervantez. The latter almost tumbled from

my lips without pause. That wouldn't have boded well for me.

Disgust mottled her flawless face. "Whatever you are, listen up. You might've been the princess from wherever you were, but this is the University of Nomadia. You are a nothing here. So, we need a last name."

"I don't have one."

She tossed the paper to the scowling, green-eyed, brown-haired man beside her. "You deal with her, Logan. I've checked in four of these freaks—a slug, a turtle, a snake, and a fucking iguana. I don't even want to *know* what this twisted bitch is."

"Stacy." Macen's voice was a husky whisper, low and growly. I didn't want to think about the warm flush of heat in my insides.

Logan checked the sheet. "Huh. There's only one left to check in, and I doubt it's you—unless you're a male ferret named Dale."

"No, afraid not."

Logan's light brown hair was cropped short. He was tall, like Macen, but thinner. Lean and sleek, but still firm in all the right places. I smirked when he winked. He was a player like a lot of the Cervantez pack I'd observed from a distance. Unlike them, though, he interacted with me. Deep green eyes danced in amusement, but not at me. No, this man grinned and chuckled *with* me.

Some of the tension left me. Not all of these people were like my pack had been. Maybe this was a new beginning. Maybe I'd fit in better. Maybe they wouldn't care that I was defective.

"Just get her gone already, Logan. Maybe Macen can help you." She glared over my shoulder. "She doesn't belong here, and I don't like the vibe I'm getting from her."

Okay, it wasn't much different from my pack. I could handle this. I could handle her. I'd dealt with worse.

"I'm really very sorry. I honestly don't know how he would've registered me. I don't even know if he did." *All he did was dump me here.*

Pain radiated within me, deep in my marrow. He'd been the closest to a father I'd been allowed. His mate, Elise, had once cared for me—showing me mercy when no one else would. The pack accepted my existence even though they all agreed I should've been destroyed.

I swallowed and tried to seal off the emotional dam threating to drown me. I was a hot mess. My emotions were all over the place. I couldn't break down, not here where people could see.

Stacy sighed and took the sheet, glancing at it one more time. "Lookit, you aren't on this one, so maybe you aren't in this category. It can be confusing, I guess."

"What are you?" Logan asked.

I hedged my response, unsure how to answer. What the hell was I? Good question. Excellent one, in fact.

"I was raised with a wolf pack."

There. Information without detail. I could do this.

C‹

Macen

The beast within me growled, demanding I do something to help this female. I'd stood and watched her Alpha break her down until she was a crumbled shell. Never interfering with an Alpha while dealing with a pack member was one of the imperative rules of my kind, yet my wolf had wanted to destroy that fucker.

I'm not a good person. I'd seen a lot of fucked-up shit. My father's pack was the fiercest in the region—arguably in the country. I didn't do the protective wolf bullshit. That was for beta pussies. I kicked ass and drew blood until my enemy submitted.

So, why did I want to drag her into a dark corner and wrap her within my embrace until she stopped trembling, and the fear I sensed drifting through her gave way to desire?

I wanted to stroke her, taste her. I wanted to bury myself in her slick heat until she screamed my name and forgot all about the bullshit she'd gone through. I'd never seen someone like her. Maybe that's why my wolf wanted to claim her.

Her ebony hair tumbled around her shoulders in curly ribbons of silk. Her skin had appeared soft, almost translucent in the sunlight. She was all curves and innocence in a petite frame—so small my wolf was afraid we'd break her.

Darkness settled in my veins when I noted the older black, yellow, and purplish bruising along her arms. The scene I'd witnessed was nothing different for her.

"Yo, man. Snap to it." Logan slapped my back. "Stop day dreaming and start dealing. You hear what Riletta said? She was raised in a pack."

"Never say that name." Her fucker of an Alpha had wielded it like a sword, slicing her each time he used it. I didn't want her equating the pain he'd created with me or anything to do with me.

"What's your problem, man?"

"Later." Logan was allowed great leniency as my second. It didn't mean I'd allow his bullshit to continue any longer. Questioning me before the pack wouldn't happen.

Ever.

A college pack was a joke. Too many Alphas in too small a space created an explosive concoction of drama and hormones with a short, pre-lit fuse. Somehow, it'd been mine to handle for three years. One more to go and I'd assume leadership of my father's pack.

I directed my attention to my wolf's obsession. She'd

retreated back into herself. Her expressive face displayed the shift in emotions, and I could taste her fear and despair. It sickened me. Stacy had cut her down and sliced her apart while I'd been distracted.

Stacy was a good female Alpha, or so I was told. Personally, I couldn't stand the bitch, but I handled her. Most assumed she'd be my mate, but I'd rather send my nuts through a meat grinder than have my wolf bound to her for eternity. No way.

I could barely fuck her when the need arose. I hated the fucking tradition of the male and female Alphas hooking up. Fortunately, she had plenty of playthings to scratch her itches.

"Logan, take over for Stacy. Which pack were you part of?" I waited for Riletta to snap back to awareness. Motioning for the binder we kept on all the packs in North America, I waited for the gorgeous dark blue eyes that spent too much time looking down. If I did nothing else while she was here, I'd make those eyes smile.

Vanessa brought the binder to me. The perky brunette rubbed against me. "Thanks, Van."

She fluttered her lashes and rubbed her front against me again in a blatant invitation. My wolf growled. The low rumble made her retreat.

The back of my neck pricked as I heard the rumble of warning coming from my pack. Dean Sandusky shoved his way through my pack, his paunch belly leading the way. The bald prick in an ill-fitting black suit was the last thing I needed right now.

He was a piece of shit. I spent more time unraveling his web of crap than I did learning shit. He'd shifted his focus to breaking down my pack. I'd figured out why—we held too much power—but I didn't have time for political bullshit.

"What are you doing here, Dean?"

"I understand there's a disturbance." His gaze roamed

Riletta with lewd interest. Miserable prick had no business thinking that shit. "You were supposed to go to my office."

"Who are you?" she asked.

"Doctor Richard Sandusky, Dean of Admissions. I knew you were trouble. I should've refused the favor asked of me and kept you away from all of these exemplary shifters of academia."

"My apologies, Doctor. I must've misunderstood."

He preened under her discomfort like the miserable virus he was. "Well, see it doesn't happen again. This is an institution of learning. We don't have time to coddle you like you're accustomed to." The dean looked at Stacy. "She'll be in Ruger Hall."

A few of the people around me gasped and distanced themselves. Fuck. Ruger Hall was the last place she belonged.

This bullshit isn't going down. I sent the thought to my pack through our telepathic link. I rarely communicated with the entire pack at once. That fact had made everyone's attention focus on the dean.

I'd labeled him a threat, and my crew took that shit seriously.

She isn't even wolf. Why are you doing this shit?

Not dealing with your melodramatics now, Stacy.

"I'm done with the freaks. Van, be a sweetheart, and take over for me. I can't deal." Stacy flounced off in a flurry of golden locks.

We've got your back, for what good it'll do. Hate to side with Blondie, but we have no jurisdiction over her since she isn't wolf.

She was raised by a pack. We'll make her history work.

We'll sort shit later. Logan flexed his fists and took a position beside me. His presence calmed my wolf somewhat, but standing here like a pussy and saying nothing wasn't working. I could see Riletta giving up. She'd stopped caring. She wanted out of here, and I couldn't blame her.

Fuck, I wanted out of this, and it wasn't my shit. One thing about wolves—we took care of our own. Her pronouncement made this our problem whether she liked it or not.

She kept retreating into the corner, away from me and my pack, as though distancing herself from our presence. Security guards appeared and surrounded her.

"We're funding her with a state run program, so her tuition and board are covered. She'll need to purchase the meal plan and her own books." The dean smirked.

Riletta's cheeks reddened. Tears pooled in her eyes.

"Miserable son of a bitch," Logan whispered.

"Why the fuck would he air this shit?"

"To break her," Logan stated.

I could feel my pack behind me. Disgruntled and pissed. Confused. The emotions all struck me.

Keep your shit together. Focus on getting this prick out of here.

I shoved the order out through our telepathic bond. It'd have to do. Visibly shaken, Van went behind the table and thumbed through papers until she came to one she turned around for Riletta to review. "Here are the plans."

She pointed at the sheet and withdrew the wad of cash I'd seen the prick shove at her in the parking lot. The paltry sum was probably all she had, and it wasn't nearly enough. What the fuck was the piece of shit thinking? The Alpha within me raged; the man within me wanted to protect her. The wolf within me wanted to destroy the son of a bitch who'd put her in this position.

"Are you sure?" Van chewed on her lower lip and patted her flat belly. "That one only covers two meals a day during the week, nothing on the weekends. You're probably used to more food since you were raised with a wolf pack. The guys eat nonstop."

"It'll be fine." She fumbled with the wad of bills, straightening them as she counted them out. Every last fucking one of them. She picked up a map of the campus and shoved it into her pocket along with her fifty bucks of change. "Thanks."

"You'll have to purchase a pass if you intend to leave campus on the weekends. Security is a priority here." The dean smirked. "Van, give her the form. We need to get her escorted to her quarters before dusk."

"Why?" she asked.

"That portion of the campus is restricted access after dusk," I stated. She didn't need to know the rest now. "As resident Alpha of the Wolf Pack, I'll offer accommodations until her paperwork is completed."

"Where? You're crammed in as it is," a guard said.

"We'll figure it out," Logan replied. "That's pack business, and you aren't pack."

"No." The dean severed all arguments to the contrary. "This isn't up for discussion. Fill out your paperwork, and pay Van the twenty dollars for the pass. We must go."

She yanked a twenty from her depleted funds and stared at the paperwork. She scrawled something on the form and returned it. I moved to stand beside Van and took the form. Blank except for her first name. Riletta.

Who was this woman?

An errant tear fell onto the sheet when I set it down on the table. A growl rolled from my gut. She smiled at Van and palmed the pass as I stood there like a neutered dog unable to stop this shit from going down.

My agitation fed the pack. I sensed the frenzy forming around me, the shift in tension was thick and palpable. Logan's voice punctured the tension.

We'll regroup tomorrow. Everyone move out.

"Perhaps there's room in Badger Hall, Dean. The renovations are finished from what I could tell," Van stated.

Because of our size, we'd assumed control over the vacant Badger Hall. It'd been a tedious process getting the building up to code since those good for nothing badgers had chewed through the insides like they'd been building freaking dams.

"Do as I said. I will not have someone of her ilk in the other halls." He motioned toward a couple of guards. One pulled a needle out. "We must begin registering your existence. It's a shame we must deal with this. Draw her blood, and then make sure she gets to Ruger Hall without causing any further problems."

"Yes, sir."

The guard shoved the needle into her arm without warning. She yelped at the invasion, tugging and pulling to escape. Growls echoed around me, but I ignored them all as I leaped over the table and dragged her away from him.

"Touch her again, and you answer to me."

Chapter Two

Riletta

I blinked the shame from my watery eyes and found myself behind a wall of sinewy flesh. When had Macen moved in front of me? Logan stood beside him. Tension blanketed the area as the two wolves stared down security. Several wolves circled behind me, sealing me within their midst.

"It's okay. I overreacted." I pulled on Macen's shirt, pleading silently for a stand down. Trouble was the last thing I could afford to create. I regarded the dean through the two motionless walls before me. "Is that all you need, Dean?"

"Yes. Let's get you locked down before nightfall."

"Wait. One more thing." Van shoved her way through to me and held out a card. "ROAR. It's a support group you can call for assistance. Anytime. They're awesome."

"Thanks." The card was heavy in my hand. Shoving it into my pocket, I headed out of the room with the dean and four security guards. The suitcase scraped along the floor, the wheels broken years ago. Conscious of the noise, I lifted it.

My gaze remained locked on the backs of the guards

before me even though the shadowed steps behind me echoed in my ears. Macen hadn't left me yet. His presence was calming, yet unsettling. The bipolar emotions left me silent. I wanted him here, but I didn't want him to get in trouble with the dean.

What pack did he come from? Where was he from? For him to be the Alpha here meant something. Even I, with my very limited knowledge, realized the entirety of the wolf students had to vote him in. I remembered that from the time Roberto had failed to make Alpha at his university.

Jacob had never forgiven his son for the shame.

"Make sure she gets to Ruger Hall. I have deserving students' business to deal with." An enormous weight lifted from me when the dean left.

"You're a stubborn little mouse."

"Stop calling me that."

"Oh, you do have a spine. I was wondering when we'd see it. No wolf should ever allow a human to speak to them like he just did."

"I'm not part of your pack, so there's no shame to you in my actions."

"You think that's the only thing I give a shit about?" His jaw twitched as he slowed his pace to accommodate my shorter stride. "You have no business in Ruger Hall."

"I have no choice."

"Bullshit. I offered you a place in our hall. Take it."

"The dean made it quite clear I was not allowed in there."

"Fuck the dean," Macen growled.

"Why can't you just leave me be?"

"I saw what went down in the parking lot." The whispered confession shredded my insides. "That prick was your Alpha?"

Nothing good would come from this conversation. We fell into a somewhat uncomfortable silence as we crossed the large campus. My legs ached; my stomach cramped.

"We're stopping." Macen settled his hand at my waist and guided me to the right.

"No stops were authorized," one of the guards stated as he touched his walkie-talkie.

"We're stopping," Macen repeated. "Keep them company."

Logan nodded at the curt command. A blur of bodies filled the area between me and the guards. Macen guided me through a door. My stomach rumbled when the succulent scent of freshly baked bread and a wide assortment of foods permeated my nostrils. Even the meat smelled good. My hands trembled when I reached for a tray.

Thirty dollars.

I could eat, and then find a store to buy supplies for the rest of the weekend. Job hunting would be a priority on Monday after the whole identity issue was sorted.

"You didn't eat lunch. I heard what he said." Macen piled food onto my tray. Salad, yogurt, cheese and fruit. "What can't you eat?"

I swallowed, my mouth salivating as I eyed the tray.

"Riles. Answer me."

"My name's Riletta."

He halted. Obsidian-laced gray eyes latched onto me, sucking me into their dark depths. His scent permeating the air between us, his hand settled on my waist. I leaned into his warmth as my skin tingled with the need for his touch. How could someone crave a touch so much? The ache stung, hurt to the point of pain.

"Don't ever ask me to use the name he brandished like a weapon. You can be the meek little mouse from the parking lot or the brief glimmer of courageous beauty I saw moments ago. You will never be that name to me."

Well. Okay. I shivered under the ferocity, the force of his words. A part of me wanted to curl into his embrace, suckle on the security and comfort he could offer.

Bad things happened when my guard went down.

I'd learned my lesson long ago.

Trembling, yet determined, I pulled away and shoved the tray forward past the wide assortment of chicken, fish, and beef. I'd never seen this much food. Okay, I had, but not for my consumption. I removed some of the items he'd placed there.

"Whoa." He covered my hand with his. "Can you eat this food?"

"Yes, but it's too much."

"Bullshit. You're a little thing, but even you can put this away easily," he whispered. "Eat an apple or the whole fucking grouping of food, and it's all the same price."

I nodded, keeping the items on the tray. I grabbed a few granola bars, some crackers, peanut butter cups, and other items I could tuck away for the coming weekend. Some cooked veggies and humus finished off my greedy grabbing. Too aware of the hoard of food I dared to take—more than I'd eaten in the past two weeks—I kept my gaze averted when the register appeared in my peripheral vision. I handed the cashier my card.

"No need for that in this hall, especially when you're with him."

"This hall?" I looked around and swallowed as my stomach lodged in my throat. He'd taken me into the private cafeteria for Wolf Hall. The sign loomed above me, a warning to all entrants this was wolf country. Restricted access. "I'm not supposed to be here."

"Come." Macen carted the tray to a table on a small second story platform. "I'll expect you here for no less than three meals this weekend. I will know if you don't show up, Riles. You don't want me coming for you."

"I'm not part of your pack. You aren't obligated to tend me." I stiffened my stance. "I can handle myself."

Setting the tray down, he studied me from the other side of the table. I shrank beneath his scrutiny until his gaze traveled downward in a slow, leisurely caress which left my skin heated and my breathing raspy.

This wasn't good. An attraction like this spelled disaster with a capital D. Cunning Alphas would use whatever hold they had on a person if given half a chance. Macen was cunning without question. I needed to sever whatever I sensed developing between us.

It was new—thrilling and exciting—yet terrifying. Sensations I'd never experienced erupted within me. Heated skin, labored breaths, hardened nipples, and a throb between my legs. I was aroused. The shock flooded me with a new wave of headiness. I wanted more of this, wanted to experience what happened after. I couldn't take the risk.

"I have no doubt you've *tended* yourself for a long time."

"Good, then we agree. I appreciate your kindness today, but I will manage well enough on my own beginning tomorrow." There. I mentally snapped the attraction tethering us together. Determination made my stomach lurch and my pulse quicken with an agitation I couldn't abate.

"We'll see, Riles. We'll see." He dragged a chair from the table and motioned. "Sit. Eat."

I inhaled the food and embraced the silence around me. Macen stood guard at the base of the second stairwell. Thankful for the moment of solitude, I steeled my nerves. Today had been a day. A bad one.

But I was free.

I swallowed more than I chewed, shoveling the food into me like a starved man on execution day. I gulped the entire glass of tea in one fast inhalation. Another appeared in front of me before I could think to ask for more.

I glanced up at the hand holding the glass and

stammered at Logan's grin. "I love a woman who knows how to eat."

The teasing tone set me at ease as I continued powering my way through my food. I'd set the bars and peanut butter and apples aside along with the crackers. Everything else was fair game. Thank goodness my stomach kept up, accepting everything with a rumble for more.

I loved this place. This food. The bread wasn't stale; the vegetables weren't on the verge of rotten. The food wasn't leftovers no one else wanted. It was mine. All mine.

Elation filled me. I was a stranger. The slate was erased, blank for new experiences. This was my chance to live normally, make friends. Sure, I wasn't in the best hall, and I had next to no money. The meal ticket was all I needed, and this was a college town. I'd find a job. I was good at a lot of things—washing dishes, scrubbing floors and toilets. I'd done it all for an entire pack. Surely, I could handle a job here, whatever it was.

I tried to swallow the belch rising from my throat, but it tumbled out freely, no doubt empowered by new mindset—one I'd achieved thanks to the brief moments of security Macen and his pack had offered. Heat rose in my cheeks when I looked over at the two men who'd dutifully sat and watched me inhale my food with the efficiency of a Hoover.

Macen's grin made my stomach flip-flop in a good way. I took a few slow sips of the sweet tea as my gaze darted over to a buffet table I hadn't seen. Desserts. A smirk appeared on his face as he rose. "Chocolate?"

I nodded, a little embarrassed. I'd packed away enough food for a rather large family already. I hadn't had devil's food cake since my fifth birthday—the last party I'd had.

Don't think about the past. Embrace the future.

"Thanks." I flashed a tentative grin at him as I picked up the fork and devoured my cake, a dueling blend of dark chocolate and something else…cherry, maybe? I ate two pieces to be precise. Jesus, this was the best shit I'd ever had. I flicked my tongue over the frosting still on the fork and glanced down at the plate longingly. I'd lick it clean, but I had to have at least a little decorum here, right?

I sucked the last bit of frosting from the fork while my gaze met Macen's. Something moved within me, caressing against the underside of my skin. I shivered as moisture pooled between my legs when I imagined tasting his skin, licking along his neck, down his chest. He'd taste better than this cake.

His nostrils flared, his eyes widening as he leaned back and mumbled, "I'll never look at cake the same ever again."

Dear God, they sensed I was turned on. How could I not remember they'd sense that even if I wasn't wolf? I'd lived with that terror most of my life—afraid my emotions would be misconstrued by the wrong person.

"Don't." Macen grabbed my hand and squeezed until my fear subsided and the warm calm returned, pooling in my limbs as though I was floating on air. "Don't ever be ashamed of what you feel, Riles. Ever."

"I didn't mean to get so excited about cake."

"It certainly makes me look at it with an all new respect," Macen teased.

"No shit." Logan stood. "Suddenly, I'm in the mood to go run. Maybe to China, possibly Australia. I'll let you know."

Had I upset them? Maybe they were too polite to speak their mind. I'd never known wolves like that, but perhaps they existed. My packed stomach was unsettled until Macen's hand rested on mine. The warmth seeped into the stinging coolness my fear had started. I didn't want to upset them. They'd been kind to me.

"Don't mind him. We're still housebreaking him."

Logan growled from halfway down the stairs. I couldn't help but laugh. Macen's eyes lit with golden flecks, his full lips turned into a grin. Yeah, this man was everything I'd sworn to never hope for and everything I wanted.

Maybe this place wasn't so bad after all. Grasping the new seeds of hope I'd planted, I stood and grabbed one of the bags from the corner of the room. Filling it with my leftovers, I breathed a small sigh of relief.

Thanks to Macen's kindness, I'd have food for the weekend. The limited funds I had wouldn't last long. I didn't know how much thirty dollars would get me, but it wouldn't be much. Then again, I was a student. I didn't need much.

I made my way down the stairs and fell into step beside Macen as we returned outside and continued the trudge to my new quarters. Each step seemed to make those around me grimmer. Clearly, there were things I had yet to figure out about Ruger Hall.

We reached a makeshift checkpoint of some sort. The guards turned and regarded Macen and his crew. "This is where you leave."

Macen palmed my face and dragged my gaze upward to lock with his. "If you need anything at all, call Wolf Hall. Or better yet, call the ROAR hotline. They'll help you."

I nodded. I didn't exactly have a phone, but I'd figure something out. He'd already done too much.

"Breakfast tomorrow." He grinned. "I almost hope you forget so I have reason to chase you."

My belly fluttered with awareness. I wasn't used to flirtation. He kissed my forehead and left.

The guards motioned for me to continue. We walked for longer than I'd expected. Darkness enveloped Ruger Hall as though the few lone rays of sunlight glimmering on the horizon couldn't break through the hall's gloom.

We stopped at the base of the structure, which sat on a hilltop on the otherwise desolate stretch of campus.

"There's a staircase to the left. You're in room two hundred twelve at the end of the hall on the right." The security guard made no move to enter. "No one from Ruger Hall is allowed beyond the entry gate we passed a few hundred yards back until dawn. If you have a problem, call the security in this dorm. This isn't our jurisdiction."

I dragged my suitcase behind me as I ignored the unease pinging along my spine.

I studied the dark entryway, the even gloomier décor—black furniture, dark gray walls offset by flickers of light from red candles. Thick, blood-red curtains covered the windows, swallowing any light. A large parlor was to the right. Ignoring it and any possible inhabitants, I made my way up the steep, narrow staircase. The stereotypical décor accomplished its purpose—to terrify the ever-living shit out of me.

My pulse quickened when I began walking down the narrower, darker hallway. The grating of unmoving plastic against worn carpet made me shudder. Goose bumps formed on my arms. Someone was watching me. Doors cracked open when I passed, but no one exited or offered a welcome. Nothing in this place screamed welcome. The dark, foreboding interior was a cliché in a Goth sort of way.

Trapped here until morning, I fought the urge to sprint from the place and find Macen. My frayed nerves screamed for a shred of normalcy. I was free from Cervantez pack restrictions. I'd waited for this moment for years, never realizing how isolating it would be.

It wasn't supposed to be like this.

I stared at the door and wondered if I should knock. Did I have a roommate? Was there a monitor I was supposed to check in with? Was there a brochure I could pick up on Roommate Etiquette 101? I'd never shared a space with another person before. What if I screwed up and pissed her off? Or worse, what if my inquisitive nature took control and I offended her? The questions ping-ponged around—lost in the void of things I didn't know. They were the least of my worries.

Shoving the mouse persona I'd embraced my entire life aside and channeling my inner Riles, I turned the nob and pushed on the door until it gave way. A lone bulb cast a pale, yellow light into a black room. Black walls, black furniture, black everything. A Goth invasion had entered and vomited its bleak décor on the small room.

"What do you want?"

A girl exited what I assumed was a bathroom. With a hand on one lean hip, she glared at me through two inches of mascara and eyeliner. Black eyes speckled with flecks of red studied me until I averted my gaze. She was thin, tall—Hell's version of a runway model.

Ruger Hall was demonic land. Few universities embraced Demonia's desire to educate their youth in Earthen ways. None of the customs and traditions ingrained in me would do any good here. I was, once again, nothing.

"I'm Riletta. Your roommate, I assume."

"Huh." She smacked blackened lips and approached. Long, blue-painted fingernails strummed against her neck, a sharp contrast to her alabaster skin. "What are you?"

"Good question."

"I thought so." She waited a moment before sighing. "You aren't gonna tell?"

I moved to the empty side of the room and set my meager belongings on the bed, taking special care to extract the pilfered fruit and crackers I'd stashed in my pockets like a squirrel gone rabid.

"You expecting an Apocalypse I need to know about?"

"Not particularly."

"Well, keep that shit on your side of the room. If I see rats or bugs because of it, you and me are gonna have issues." She flashed a set of fangs and shrugged into a leather jacket. "So, what the hell are you?"

"Don't know; don't care." Indifference seemed the best defense. "What are you?"

"Half vampire, half demon. I was raised in the Earthen dimension, which is why they seemed to think I could deal with your ass when we got stuck with you. Totally *not* cool. So keep your shit on your side, and don't get in my business."

"Okay."

"You know anything about Ruger Hall?"

I shook my head and unzipped my suitcase, trying to focus on anything aside from the furious pumping of my blood. Demons. I knew nothing about Demonia. I was ignorant about cultural beliefs, dietary needs. I was totally unsuited for my new surroundings.

"I can practically taste your fear. That's some really strong shit for my kind. You're best sticking to the room for the first couple of months. This wing is all freshmen. Most of them just got here from Demonia where you'd be an appetizer before the feast."

Great.

"We all signed agreements not to bite or feed, but that wouldn't stop the succubus demons from whipping you into frenzy and getting drunk off your fear. I'd almost pay money to see that shit." She wedged her feet into combat boots and stood fully. "You always glimmer?"

"I glimmer?"

"Maybe it's the lighting on your pale-ass skin." She shrugged. "I'm light, but you give a whole new meaning to the term, you know?"

"I guess."

"Whatever." She grabbed a set of keys from a peg at

the door. "Just so you know, it's gonna suck ass for you here. Our classes are all at night, so the rest of the campus can breathe easy and not be around us. We're too cool to hang with their shitty asses anyway.

"Summation for you—we're loud and in charge at night. You aren't shit. Stay in the room and I'll try to keep them from messing with you as long as you don't piss me off. Got me?"

"Yeah." I would've agreed to anything to get her gone. I needed time alone to think, figure out what I was going to do—if there was anything I could do.

It wasn't like I had a treasure-trove of resources at my disposal. The card Van had offered. It was a hotline of some sort. Maybe they could offer some advice. It couldn't hurt. "Is there a phone around here?"

"You believe cell phones rot our brains?"

"No, just can't afford one."

"Whatever. It's on the desk over here. It's routed to Demonia, so don't go calling Kansas."

"I'm not from Kansas."

She turned and shook her head. "What do you shift into?"

"I can't shift."

"So, you're not a shifter."

"I am. I think. I just don't shift."

"I could bite you if you want to know. I could taste what you are in your blood. Maybe. It's been awhile since I've gotten to bite anyone. Wanna try?" The hopeful lilt in her voice pinged my *oh shit* meter into the red.

"No thanks." I reversed until the backs of my knees thumped against the bed. "Appreciate it, though."

"Whatever." She rubbed her temples. "I've already got a headache twenty minutes into dealing with your ass. I deserve a bump in my grades or a cut of the money the dean got to take you in."

"Have fun."

She turned the nob and froze in the doorway. Turning to face me, she glared. "You're going to sit here and get mopey and weepy and shit. I can't stand that shit—makes the back of my mouth bitter and my sinuses swell."

"Sorry."

"That's it." She slammed the door while on the wrong side. I wanted her gone. "Get some decent clothes on. You're going to Temple with me."

Temple didn't sound like a place I wanted to go. "No thanks."

"Not an option. You, sitting here, sorting your mental shit is gonna make me sick when I get back. It'll ooze into the vents and get everyone around us fucked up, too, and I ain't putting up with their crap 'cause you're all weepy and shit. Got me?"

I didn't respond. What could I say? Tears burned the back of my eyes, and I tasted the screams in my throat. I was terrified, pissed, and confused. I was lonely, desperate, and, did I mention, terrified out of my ever-living, fucking mind? Oh, yeah, and I was a little sick of being everyone's chew toy.

"That's more like it." She smirked as she focused on my suitcase. "Keep the last thought, whatever it was. Own it, make it your bitch. Live it tonight, and you might actually make it a week in Ruger. You've got some serious mojo when you channel it."

She fished through my clothes, tossing them into two heaps on the floor at the end of the bed. "I've had cleaning rags with more style than this crap. Newer, too. You wear this shit?"

"Sorry, Gucci wasn't on my route here."

"Smart ass doesn't suit you, Princess Barbie."

"My name's Riletta."

"Whatever." She grabbed a T-shirt from her drawer and tossed it to me. "Throw this on so they won't give me shit."

I complied, pretty sure I wasn't going with her.

"And don't even think about not going. Five minutes alone and everyone in a half mile radius will sense your breakdown. You're like the last crack pipe in a room full of addicts."

"So, you're taking me to this temple where they all are anyway? How will that help?"

"You focus on your shit, and we taste it. You focus on ours, and you're just a princess out of place—a curiosity we'll want to gnaw on, but we'll eventually spit you out."

"Lovely."

"I thought so." She opened the door after I'd donned the shirt. "Let's move."

"I don't think this is a good idea. I'm not an overly religious person."

"Cute." She laughed. "Look, you come and show your face so I don't deal with the questions about your ass for a week, and I'll get your innocent Princess Barbie ass home so you can crash. You keep your shit together for the next few days, and I'll get you alone where you can sort your ass however you want. We good?"

We were so *not* good. I nodded anyway. "I don't even know your name."

She didn't respond until we were outside and standing beside a large Harley Davidson motorcycle. Sleek black mingled with fiery orange flame work. It was hot and dangerous, much like the woman.

Yeah, I was totally crushing on her bad ass persona. Why couldn't I be more like her? Were there classes I could take? Bad Ass 101 perhaps?

She straddled the bike with a gruff, "Get on."

I'd never been on a motorcycle, but didn't think she was in the mood to know that. Over the years, I'd learned when to shut it, and this was most certainly one of those moments.

The machine purred and growled beneath us like a

primal beast waiting to be tamed. It reminded me of Macen in a lot of ways. My pulse quickened beneath my skin. Something within me lapped up the sensations, reveling in the freeness of the dark cloaking us.

"Yeah, you aren't weepy any more, are you?" She chuckled. "Name's Vira."

"Like Elvira?"

"Only if you want to feel your blood being drained until you crumple at my feet."

"Definitely not Elvira, then."

"Thought so."

I grabbed onto her jacket, unsure exactly how I was supposed to hold on. Wrapping my arms around another woman wasn't gonna happen—not that I had any problems with that sort of thing. It just wasn't me.

"There's a handle behind you. Lean back and reach."

Fortunately, the destination was close—since we cut through a freaking *cemetery*. I'd barely settled into the hum between my legs before we stopped, and I was guided into an abandoned church. Bass vibrated the windows as we entered. Flickers of red and blue arrowed a few dim rays of light into an otherwise darkened room. Gregorian style chants filled the air, echoing in the large gutted hall. The stench of stale cigarette smoke, sweat, and alcohol permeated the area. I grimaced at the aroma as I followed Vira into God only knew what.

Chapter Three

Macen

The crowd gyrated in time to the sensual Gregorian style chants—the deep soothing baritones ripe with a double entendre which wrapped me within its depths and beckoned me to join the enfolding crush of bodies. I envisioned silken ebony curls brushing across my skin as Riles's legs wrapped around me.

I needed to get laid.

Temple was neutral ground on the edge of the Demonia-run portion of campus and ours. Although my pack frequented this place, my presence was rarely welcomed.

"You get it set up?"

"Yeah." Logan motioned toward a darkened corner of the room. "Meeting's going down over there. You sure about this?"

"We have a choice?"

"Kicking his miserable ass like you usually do seems like a good idea to me."

"You heard what he said."

"I'd like to see him try and pull it off. Whatever she is, she's not under their sanction. She couldn't be. She's the sweetest, most innocent piece of—"

"Finish that, and you're the one in the ring with me tonight." My wolf edged closer, yearning to be unleashed. Five minutes alone with the miserable Alpha hellhound, and all would be good.

Too bad Diego didn't play clean.

"Well, well, well. If it isn't the infamous, soon-to-be Alpha of the Giordano pack. To what do I owe this astute pleasure?"

"Cut your shit, Diego. Let's get this done."

He sighed and cracked his knuckles as he smirked at the goon to his left. "We're waiting on a couple of guests. There's no reason to rush this. We have all night."

Bullshit. My beast was on a short leash that we were here settling this recent round of crap. Diego and I had danced this fucking tune a few too many times for my taste, and even though I was more than ready to make his beat down a permanent one, I knew better.

Dean Richardson appeared from the shadows with a gleam of amusement on his face. Logan growled beside me.

"What's the meaning of this meeting?" the dean asked.

"You know damned good and well what the meaning is. Tell me why you put Riletta in Ruger Hall. This isn't going down. You feel me?"

"How is this unknown shifter your concern, wolf?" Diego shrugged. "I'll make sure to *personally* take *real good* care of her."

I lunged, my weight pulled back by Logan when he gripped my shoulders. "Touch her, and you die."

Not smart, man. Give him leverage, and he'll use it.

Too late. Diego's smug grin returned.

"Interesting."

Fuck. I ran my hand through my hair and forced my wolf to calm. We both knew why I was here—to ensure her safety in Ruger Hall. Bad shit went down on a daily basis. A non-demon had no business there.

"What do you want? Name it."

"A challenge fight next Friday. Here at Temple."

I'd known the price. It was sheer lunacy to even consider because of the underlying understanding. I had to lose. No Alpha would willfully submit to another, become a worthless bitch before their entire pack. I doubted my wolf would handle the price, but I'd agree to anything to secure her even if it was for a little while. I'd deal with the reality later when it came.

A week was a fuck of a long time for things to change. We'd figure something out before then.

"Forget it," Logan growled.

"Done," I responded.

Notify Lane I need him to get his ass off vacation. Thinking the pack may want a new Alpha if shit goes south Friday.

That shit's not going down.

My call. I shifted on the balls of my feet, silently begging for the miserable hellhound to fuck up.

Diego smirked. "Should I spell out my expectations?"

"No." I couldn't handle any of that shit now.

Challenges between the hellhound and me had become an expected sport on campus. We'd been ripping each other apart on a regular basis for the past three years, and the prick had yet to make my ass submit in the ring.

I'd made him howl like a bitch repeatedly.

Fuck, this shit sucked. Riles wasn't my problem, but there was no way my wolf would turn away from her now. He'd bought into the meek, little mouse.

We'll figure things out later. This gives us time.

"Understand this, hellhound. One hair on her head gets so much as moved, and you'll suck food via a straw up your ass. That's how jacked I'll leave you after I'm done. You feel me?"

I needed to get out of this steaming sewer. My wolf

needed to run. Maybe fuck every willing female in a five mile radius. Not that it'd do a lick of good. All I could think about was sinking my dick into Riles.

I'd heard that was possible—where your dick grew a brain and decided unilaterally only one woman would do. Totally fucked up. I wasn't ready for a connection that permanent, but my wolf was definitely in charge of my dick's decision.

I turned to leave, but my peripheral vision latched onto the dean. I prowled forward and leaned into him until the miserable excuse for a human trembled. "You and I are going to tango soon."

Diego wouldn't cover his ass beyond tonight. If nothing else came from this cluster fuck, at least the pathetic excuse for a dean would be handled. One less hassle to deal with later.

Fuck, it was a pain in the ass to be Alpha.

I shoved my way through the swelling mass of grinding bodies, ignoring the roaming hands running along my torso. Female demons were a lot like bitches in heat—except they had no off switch. Normally, I played along with them, feeding them the sexual vibes they craved.

Not tonight.

Tonight, I needed to get the fuck out of here and run. Eat up some earth beneath my paws and howl into the darkened night until my throat burned and I purged the rage and animosity I'd been chewing on.

"Hey, wolf. I heard you were here. Figured I'd cash out the favor I owe you."

I sighed and looked around for Logan. Where the fuck was he? I'd hoped he'd keep these demon bitches away from me. I was on a frayed leash right now.

"Not now."

"You sure?"

I turned my attention to the demon. "Ah. The

cemetery debacle. I remember now."

"Like I said, I'm cashing out my favor to you." Her jaw twitched.

"Who said I wanted you to?"

She shrugged. "Fine. I'm sure your innocent little *Riletta* will be more than fine with a new roomie. I heard they needed a fresh slab of freshman meat up in the senior demon wing. Still not sure what happened to the last assistant they had. I'm sure she'll turn up. Eventually."

"You're rooming with Riles?" I hadn't realized I'd grabbed her throat until her fingernails flexed on my wrists. I loosened my grip. "Tell me."

"Yes. Word ran through Ruger late last night that fresh meat was being given to us. Dean Dick wanted an example made of her, something about not appreciating favors being called in."

"And you got involved how?"

"I ignored it, didn't give a rat's ass about some freak. Then word got around about registration, how he pulled shit, and you stepped in. I figured she was on your radar for a reason. I made room for her in my pad and figured I'd cash out."

"Yeah, well. You get her back, and we're good."

Vira. She'd been cornered by Diego and his crew of hellhounds at the cemetery a few months back. The boys and I had stepped in. We wouldn't let females get handled like playthings—not even in the Demonia section of the campus.

"Why are you here if she's there?"

"'Cause I brought her here." Vira put a hand on her hip and glared up at me. "Don't pull that Alpha what-the-fuck attitude with me, wolf. She was losing her shit in a wing full of succubi who literally just got off the boat from Demonia."

"So, you bring her to a club filled with them?"

"Until you get this shit sorted, she's gonna have to

deal. Losing the innocent fuzz around her aura will go a long way to making this fucked up living situation work."

"Where is she?"

"What the fuck ever," Vira sighed.

"Where?"

Vira motioned toward a darkened corner across the room. I shoved and carved a path toward her. Need channeled my blood southward. She huddled in the corner, her shock evident as her gaze flashed from one writhing couple to another.

Part of me wanted to drag her from here and tuck her into bed, let the dregs of her shitty day give way to the exhaustion I could see on her face. Her shoulders drooped as she leaned against the wall. The blood pumping downward demanded I drag her to my bed, spread her out like a feast, and dine on her until we both collapsed.

Diego would set up an ice cream stand in Demonia before that happened. Her hands trembled as she ran them down the tee she'd obviously borrowed from Vira.

"'Bite Me' doesn't seem like a motto you'd be down for. Am I wrong?"

"Is that what it says?" Her eyes widened, a sexy pink darkening her cheeks.

"I take it you don't know the language?"

"That explains all the vampires asking me to dance."

I chuckled even though my wolf prowled, ready to take on any vamp stupid enough to flash his fangs around me. I closed the distance between us and lowered my voice. The sweet succulence of lavender and rose petals filled my nostrils.

"Dance with me, mouse."

I followed the movement in her throat when she placed a hand on my arm then withdrew it quickly as though gauging my reaction. Her skin was soft, yet colder than I'd expected when I settled her hand on my chest.

She shivered when I grasped her waist and pulled until

she leaned into me rather than the cold concrete wall. Music pulsated around us, but the darkness held reality at bay.

"I think I prefer Riles."

"Me, too, sweetheart. Me, too."

Riles

This wasn't happening.

The darkness wrapped me in a warm cocoon. Hot breath fanned my cheek, the scent of male wolf filling my nostrils. My skin burned beneath his touch when his fingers fanned across my neck and down my arms.

I followed his lead, shifting my weight from one foot to the other. Dancing was new to me, and I was sure he realized that since I found his feet more often than the floor. But he said nothing.

The silence calmed me, soothed the wars within my mind. Nothing else mattered. All that existed was me and this strange, strange wolf who'd shoved his way into my life with a ferocious intensity which, quite frankly, scared the ever-living shit out of me.

I wasn't used to Alphas like him taking notice of me. He'd prowled to me, impervious to the females vying for his attention. What the hell did he want? Because it couldn't be me.

My steps faltered again. He pulled me closer, running his hands along my back until I leaned into him fully and settled my head against his shoulder. Heat smoldered between us. His muscles flexed beneath my hand—the hand I had yet to move from where he'd set it earlier. I was lost in a sea of new sensations, and I didn't care.

I wanted to know more, try to understand for myself what Macen wanted. I pulled away to capture his gaze and was momentarily trapped. Jesus, he was too much.

"What are you thinking, Riles?" he whispered.

"I'm trying to figure you out."

"Good luck with that."

"You're a senior?"

"Yeah, got started a little bit later like most shifters. Didn't get here till I was twenty. Leaving the pack was tough."

"I'd imagine so."

"How old are you?"

"Twenty." I returned my head to his shoulder. "I think. I was abandoned as a child. They weren't sure how old I was exactly. They figured I was around two. Maybe three."

"It didn't look like your Alpha did right by you."

I tensed. Jacob deserved my defense. He'd sheltered, clothed, and fed me for over eighteen years. "I'm eternally grateful for his help. He didn't have to take on the burden of my care, but he did."

"You could never be a burden."

"You'd be surprised," I whispered. I didn't like this turn of conversation. Tension corded in my back, in my limbs.

"Tomorrow, we'll call ROAR and discuss the blood they drew today. The dean can't be trusted."

"I don't think it'll do any good. Ja.... My Alpha had me tested several times. Nothing ever came of it."

"We'll see what ROAR says. They're good people."

"Why are you bothering with all this? I'm not your problem."

"You became mine the second I saw you in the parking lot. You became my wolf's sole existence when your prick of an Alpha shook you until your teeth rattled." His hands tightened at my waist, pulling me into the hard length of his body. "I'm warning you now, Riles. I've got a short leash on my wolf when it comes to you. I held him back in the parking lot. It won't happen again."

"W-what does that mean?"

48

He chuckled softly, his hot breath trailing across my ear. Deft fingers drifted through my hair and moved to expose my neck. His lips feathered across my skin, making my entire body shudder with need.

"I feel your pulse pounding, so fast and strong. I smell your arousal, and it fires my blood. Gotta confess, that makes me harder than shit."

I gasped. Heat flooded my veins, surged within me. Unsure how to respond, I remained silent in his embrace. I was nowhere near prepared for Macen, but there was no way I was backing away, running like the scared mouse he'd seen in the parking lot.

I'd dreamed of freedom for years. Was it rash to trust Macen this soon? Yes.

But I didn't care.

I had nothing.

No money, no pack. No future beyond what I could carve out at this university. In a freaking demon hall with a half-demon, half-vampire as a roommate.

Macen was the least of my problems.

He was my breath of life, freedom, and desire. I intended to inhale whenever I could, no matter the risk. He was my first taste of independence.

"Take me out of here," I whispered as I dared to move my hand to his shoulder then down his hard, muscular back. I wanted to bury my fingernails there, mark him as mine even if only for a moment.

He tensed, and my stomach lurched into my throat. I worked to extract myself from his embrace, but he wouldn't budge. My breath quickened as heat rose in my face. I was so stupid. I shouldn't have said that. What had I been thinking?

"I should get back to my dorm. I have a lot to do."

He studied me for a minute. The perusal unnerved me. Thanks to my light complexion, I wore my embarrassment like a neon flashlight despite the darkness.

"Let's go."

I nodded. Loss engulfed me when I dutifully followed him. He had better things—or rather, better people—to do. The air had grown crisp. It cooled my overheated skin when we exited the building. Couples in various states of undress writhed in time to the music drifting from the open door and windows.

He headed toward a row of motorcycles in the same area where Vira had parked hers when we arrived. His stride was long and fast—impossible for me to keep up with. I surrendered to my shorter stature and the exhaustion plaguing my limbs.

As long as I could still see him, I was okay. I understood what he was doing. Physical distance reminded me of the emotional distance he demanded. I got that. Hell, I'd lived my entire life with that distance. A one-room cottage with a bathroom on the edge of town had been my life since I was twelve.

I could handle a few feet.

He straddled a Harley at the end of the row. A moment of insecurity kept me frozen beside the massive machine. Riding behind Vira was one thing. My gaze roamed across his bulging thighs and up to his chest. He was not Vira.

"Get on before I lose it, Riles." His voice was coarse, like sandpaper across my body. I'd upset him.

Reading situations had never been a strong suit. I'd always blamed lack of experience. I owed him an apology because I'd clearly misread the vibe between us. He'd been so kind. He didn't need my emotional diarrhea.

I got on behind him and settled into the seat. Reaching behind me, I realized there was no bar to hold.

"Wrap around me, Riles."

I complied and suppressed my moan as the motorcycle rumbled to life beneath me. The thunderous grind of the machine mirrored my thoughts of him. I tried to ignore the corded muscle beneath my hands as he guided us through the cemetery. I squeezed my thighs against him with each turn.

This was hell.

I wasn't stupid. Sure, I was naïve, but I was aroused. My pulse floundered like a goldfish out of water. My heart beat like a drunken drummer, and I was very thankful I'd worn pants because bits I didn't even know could feel *at all* were throbbing with an achy need I'd never experienced.

He guided the motorcycle behind a large crypt toward the center of the cemetery. I unlatched my barnacle-like grip when he shut the engine off. Uncertain why he'd stopped, I forced some distance between us and swung off.

Macen reached out and pulled me toward him. Startled, I gasped when I fell into his lap. He grasped me in a firm hold at the base of my neck. My heart pounded wildly. Heat pooled between my legs. Closing my eyes, I pretended this was like one of those situations I'd seen some of the females from my pack in—where the male asserted his control and claim.

Wet heat swept across my lips. I trembled, unsure if the contact was real or just imagined. My eyes fluttered open, and I drowned in the arousal within his gaze.

Our breaths intermingled. I feathered my lips against his, repeating the soft sweep he'd just used. A groan escaped him, and I jumped backward, unsure if I'd done something wrong.

His grip in my hair tightened, and he growled as his mouth crushed against mine. His tongue swept across my parted lips and delved inside. The kiss was hot, demanding, and everything I'd ever desired.

I followed his commanding lead, relaxing against him. His free hand ran along my side, down my leg. I lost track of it as he guided me into an aroused frenzy with the kiss.

He pulled me from his mouth. My ragged breathing matched his. I groaned and moved to kiss him again, but he held me away and closed his eyes.

"You have no idea how easily you unleash my wolf. I vowed to do the right thing by you tonight, but I'm not a good man, Riles. I'm not what you need."

Yes, you are.

I didn't realize I'd responded aloud until he dragged me and made me straddle his lap on the motorcycle. The new position ground me against him, the prominent bulge slid nicely against the achy part of me. He nibbled on my ear, kissing behind the lobe until I shivered.

He stroked my breasts. His thumb scraped against my hardened nipple, and I gasped, thrusting myself toward him. I groaned my frustration. It was too much, yet not enough all at once. I ached and throbbed.

"Ssh. Let me have you."

Macen kissed me, the contact sweet and sultry. He licked my lips and then forayed across my tongue. Deft fingers lifted my bra and cupped my exposed breast.

I should stop this. I was in a freaking cemetery behind a crypt, letting a man I'd just met race past first base and straight to whatever-the-hell he wanted. I sensed him pulling away from the kiss, so I grabbed his head, forcing him back to where I wanted.

He tasted like fiery cinnamon. I wanted to savor every inch of his golden skin but refused to sever the contact. Alphas preferred assertive, experienced women.

He tugged my hair until I stilled. I dug my nails into his forearms and deepened the kiss. My hips ground against him. Pleasure tingled within me. I repeated it, harder this time.

"Christ, you're killing me." His hand abandoned my breast and drifted downward to my jeans. I gasped when he undid the clasp. "Let me have you, mouse."

The repeated plea left me weakened, wanton for his touch. He trailed down the expanse of exposed belly and maneuvered beneath my panties. I gasped as he found where my need pulsated.

"You're so wet for me." Hot breath fanned my neck.

I clung to him, my eyes closed, and my lips parted. Pleasure cascaded through me when his fingers began moving against me, in me. I gasped when they entered. The tender strokes made my entire body tremble with need. Breathing proved difficult, damn near impossible.

Macen held me in place with one firm hand and worked me into a fever pitch. I buried my face in his neck, inhaling his scent. Heated, musky woods. I could live buried in his scent for eternity and never complain.

I blinked through tears and abandoned myself to the sensations bursting within me. Collapsing against him, I allowed the exhaustion free rein as I rode the waves of pleasure.

Macen placed chaste kisses along my cheek, across my lips. He licked an errant tear away. The concern in his gaze made my breathing halt. I swallowed, silently praying my voice worked.

"Thank you."

"You have no idea how beautiful you are, mouse. Thank you for trusting me with this, with you." Macen set me up and helped me adjust my clothing. "Let's get you to the dorm before I forget I'm being good tonight."

If this was Macen being good, I couldn't wait to see him being bad.

Chapter Four

Riles

I gave up the concept of sleep shortly after eight the next morning. Adapting to my new environment would take some time. I'd also learned leaving Temple without telling Vira was a big no-no.

None of those things could tame the giddiness within me. I could still feel Macen's kiss against my lips as I made my way to the cafeteria. I'd planned to munch on my stored wares, but he'd made me promise to meet him there for breakfast.

I was having breakfast with Macen.

My insides zinged with a renewed sense of purpose. Suddenly, being abandoned by my Alpha and dropped off at a university to fend for myself wasn't a big deal. I'd contacted ROAR somewhere between the four a.m. bong blitz and the five a.m. blood raid. The latter still terrified the shit out of me.

I shuddered at how close I'd come to losing a few pints last night. Thank God Vira had defended me, despite being pissed about the whole leaving on the wrong Harley thing. She apparently had serious mojo because she had even the seniors quaking in their fangs when she was done with them. ROAR was all over tracking down the blood the dean had taken, not that it'd do a lot of good.

They were also going to see if they could do anything about my dorm situation. Not to be judgmental, but I was totally not a freak when compared to the peeps in Ruger Hall. The walk to Wolf Hall was longer than I'd remembered from yesterday. Maybe it was just because I was looking forward to seeing Macen. I'd chastised myself several times today already.

I was growing too attached to him too fast. It was the wolf way, but I wasn't a wolf. I had no excuse aside from the desire to not drown in loneliness again. He was an addiction—a lifeline to a real life. And a great kisser.

Nervousness returned when I entered the cafeteria, which was bustling with activity. I searched the thickening mass of people for Macen or any familiar face. Nothing.

Okay. I could do this. I got into the long line and grabbed a tray. I grabbed a couple of apples for later, along with some yogurt, toast, and oatmeal. Orange juice and milk finished off my selections.

"How did you get in here?" A petite blonde pushed my shoulder and tried to intimidate me with a growl as she stepped into my personal space.

I figured a smartass response like, "through the door" would ensure an ass kicking, which wasn't what I wanted to handle this morning. Looking around, I noticed quite a few people had stopped to watch the scene play out.

Great.

Knowing who she was and her role in the pack would go a hell of a long way to resolving this, but knowledge was power, and I never found myself with any of that. Looking around for a familiar face one more time, I realized I was on my own.

"I'm sorry. I think there's been some confusion. I was invited."

"Invited? By who?" Her voice rose.

"Missy, chill. It's cool. She's Macen's new project." The words sliced through me like a sharp, well-honed blade. Stacy appeared beside me, her blonde hair up in a ponytail which swished as she swayed her ass. "Come on, Riletta. You can sit with us. Macen and the guys had to handle some pack business, so they'll be delayed."

She grabbed my tray and sashayed through the tables, heading up the stairs to the table I'd sat at before. She set my food down and sat directly across from me. I didn't like having my back to the stairs, but I didn't have much of a choice. A mixture of men and women I didn't know regarded me with curiosity. Van smiled and waved from the other side of the long table.

Missy crowded in beside me, tossing a few glares my direction for good measure. Stacy eyed the food on my tray as she picked at her fruit.

"I wish I had the metabolism to carry off that many carbs so early in the morning. That's the bitch about being the Alpha female—I need to watch my hips and ass. Macen doesn't like a lot of padding getting in his way." She smirked when I almost knocked my juice over.

"Funny you say that, Stace, because I can think of quite a few things Macen doesn't like about you. I've never heard him complain about padding on women," Van commented as she sipped on her coffee. "Maybe we should ask him, just to be sure."

The toast was dry in my mouth. I chewed and set the half-eaten piece on my plate. I shouldn't have come here.

"So, Riletta, did you enjoy Temple last night? Those demons sure know how to throw a good party," Stacy chuckled. "We were going to look for you, but I guess you got taken out before the real fun started. It's a shame Macen didn't let you stay longer. He must be tired of special projects by now."

The repeated reference grated my nerves. I swallowed the food lodged in my throat. "Project?"

She sighed and looked at me with sad eyes. "It's really so tragically cruel. I've told him time and time again not to string girls like you along, but he really is such a kind-hearted Alpha. He can't stand to see lonely shifters in need. He's got a really bad case of what I call White Knight Syndrome."

"He was very kind, and I immensely appreciated his help yesterday." I wiped my mouth and shoved my apples into the pack I'd set on the floor beside me. Suddenly, the oatmeal and yogurt weren't that palatable.

I'd dealt with female wolves like her all my life. Discomfort only heightened the feeding frenzy like dumping a bucket of chum into shark infested waters. I ignored the digs, but they infected me. They speared me with barbs of negativity I couldn't help but believe.

I was nothing. Defective. Yet Macen had been kind to me. Did that make me a project?

"Kindness is one thing. What he does is so cruel. And clichéd." Stacy smirked and looked over at Missy. "I mean how many times have we told him to stop dragging his projects away from Temple and taking them to the crypt. It's so pathetic."

Bull's-eye.

The table erupted into laughter. Heat rose in my face, and my stomach roiled. I sat there, unsure how to eject myself from the latest nightmare. I knew better than to believe everything people said, yet this made clear sense to me. It explained the inexplicable fantasy I'd latched onto.

Knowing grins and smirks spread around the table. Van looked pained.

"Whatever Macen does isn't my business. I'm not even part of the pack. It has nothing to do with me." I forced a few sips of juice down as I strengthened the fortress I'd constructed around me over the years. "I'm just thankful you all were so kind to me yesterday."

"Yes, well, I'm sure it's difficult not knowing what you are. Not having anyone who really wants you around." Missy sighed. "I don't know how you can even stand to be out and about. I'd be so ashamed if I couldn't shift. That's just so tragic."

"At least your pack set you up here before they kicked you out," someone stated. "It isn't like you can get a job or anything since you don't have paperwork."

I hadn't even considered the no paperwork problem. I'd done some research on Vira's computer that morning. ROAR's website was packed with valuable information. I had no social security number, no identity. I didn't even have a birth certificate. All shifters were also required to have bloodwork and genetic mapping to identify their pack of origin. Without Jacob's backing, they could declare me a rogue—I'd be thrown out of the university and the human populace. Then what would I do?

Maybe ROAR could help me. I'd already downloaded and printed all the forms I thought I'd need—which, mental note, was not a good thing to do at the crack of dawn when rooming with a half vampire, half demon. She'd been a smidge cranky, but how was I to know the printer was that loud?

"How was your first night at Ruger?" Stacy asked as she reached across the table and touched my hand.

I pulled it away. "Fine. A bed is a bed. I don't care where it is. Like you said, I'm just thankful to be here."

Silence thickened the tension blanketing me for a few moments before I pushed my chair back and grabbed my backpack. "If you'll excuse me, I think I'll head back and get my things situated. Things were so stressful yesterday, I'm afraid I didn't get much handled."

"Oh, yesterday was just so wretched. It took me hours to get Macen settled last night after Temple. He was almost impossible to handle all by myself." Stacy looked down at the tray. "You sure you don't want to take a doggie bag?"

"I'm sure Macen will be along soon," Missy added. "I know he got a late start this morning."

"That was kind of my fault." Stacy blushed.

The table laughed.

"Please extend my gratitude to him when you see him." I smiled as I stood on shaky knees. "Thanks again. I'll see y'all around campus, I'm sure."

"Looking forward to it." Stacy's sing-songy voice shredded the last of my patience.

Someone called my name and chased me, but I didn't care. My sole mission was to get out of the cafeteria without further problems. What had I been thinking?

"Riletta, wait." The plea made me walk faster.

I spotted the exit and sniffled. My nostrils burned, my eyes watered, but I refused to break down here where they would see the pain their direct hits to my ego had created. I wouldn't give them the satisfaction even though I deserved it. I'd been foolish, too trusting. I'd known better.

I pushed the door open and raced down the steps, turning toward Ruger Hall. At least everyone there would be asleep. I'd be alone.

"Logan, stop her." The shouted order drew me to a halt as the lower half of a massive body appeared in my downward cast gaze.

Great.

I sighed and drew my arms around myself as I regarded the man I was pretty sure was Macen's second. Logan's gentle smile did little to ease the pain streaming through me in tidal waves, threatening to burst from me at any moment.

I needed to get away.

Labored breathing sounded behind me. I didn't bother looking because I'd recognized the voice. Van grabbed my arm and bent over.

"Shit, she can run."

"Maybe you need to stretch your wolf more often," Logan suggested. He ran a cautious gaze down me, seeing far more than I wanted him to. It was in his tone. "Riles. This is an unexpected pleasure. I hadn't expected to see you out here. Macen sent Lane and me to keep you company until he finished with pack business."

Lane was a brute of a man who towered over me. He was all coal-black hair, light blue eyes, golden skin, and a powerful, sleek grace which reminded me more of a panther than a wolf. He offered a half-grin and a chin nod as he folded his arms in front of him.

"Lane here just got back to campus after being away for a few weeks. I was getting him situated, which delayed me a few minutes. What's up, Van?" he asked.

"Thanks for the assist, boys. I'll take it from here." She pulled on my arm, but I shoved her hand away.

"I'm afraid I must pass. It's been a pleasure, but I really must go." I took a shaky breath and swiped at the unwanted moisture appearing on my cheek. "Thank you, though. Have a good day."

Sidestepping the two men in front of me, I charged down the path, my heart heavy. I didn't want the confrontation, the awkward and unnecessary reiteration.

Stacy was a cow bitch in wolf form, but she'd done me a favor—she'd set me straight with a swift, brutal knock to my ego. I'd had zero right to think I belonged at Wolf Hall even as a guest.

"Riletta, please. Just hear me out."

I stopped, unable to walk away. For some screwy reason, I wanted—no, needed—to hear her out.

"Don't call her that," Logan growled. "It's Riles."

"Whatever." She took a deep breath and glared at the two men. "Where the fuck have you been, anyway? You have no idea what the hell went down because you two oafs were sleeping in."

"Look here, little wolf. I'll take you over my knee and spank that sweet ass of yours until you learn exactly when is the only time I allow females to get all growly." Lane seized Van's hair and pulled until she cast her gaze downward in supplication.

Holy shit. My heart palpitated as I watched the exchange, my pulse racing as I wondered what she was thinking right about now. I couldn't imagine a man doing that to me, commanding my submission with such swift efficiency.

Memories of last night rushed to the forefront. Macen had been somewhat dominant but nothing like this. Heat pooled between my legs as I imagined him doing that with me.

"Explain." Lane's terse order yanked me back to reality.

"Stacy's there with her crew, and—"

"We got the picture." Logan took my arm and motioned toward the cafeteria I'd retreated from. "You eat?"

"Yes."

"No," Van argued. "It got ugly real quick."

Silence descended, but I sensed a conversation in play. I'd observed many while in Jacob's pack. The shifting facial expressions, the noted growls or grunts in response. Uneasy with them chatting about me, I tried to extract myself from their presence.

"Let's go eat."

"I'm not hungry, but thanks." My traitorous stomach growled.

Logan chuckled. "Perhaps we need to discuss honesty afterward."

I sighed my resignation as the two oafs led Van and me back into the cafeteria. The atmosphere shifted when they entered with me in tow. I ignored the whispers echoing through the room as Logan and Lane settled me between them in the line.

"I'm really not hungry. Honestly. I ate toast."

"Yeah, like a quarter piece of bread is enough for a shifter," Van commented.

"I'm not a shifter."

"You grew up with a pack. You eat like pack," Lane stated.

Arguing only opened up an entirely different can of worms I had no intention of airing. Food began appearing on my tray as the two guys settled stuff on there. I hoped this was for them because I couldn't handle the pile of stuff they were mounting.

"No meat," Logan said.

"I remember."

He remembered? How did he know? I hadn't met Lane before. For that matter, how did Logan know? I was too distracted with the impending train wreck which was the second floor to worry about that right now. We bypassed the register entirely—which made me wonder why it even existed since no one respected the card thingies anyway.

Wolves.

We trudged up the stairs, and the buzzards picking away at my gut returned swiftly, swooping in the moment my gaze captured Stacy's. Her blue eyes widened, a few gasps rose around her. Chairs shifted, trays disappeared as several of the table's inhabitants stood to leave.

"Sit." Logan's booming voice echoed off the walls.

Lane set my tray down at a seat and claimed the one to my right. Logan paused to my left, where Missy sat.

"Move."

"I was actually about to leave." The girl jumped slightly and moved a couple of seats over.

"No. You stay. You all stay." Logan placed a napkin into his lap and looked over at me. "We shall have breakfast together like a civilized pack."

"Well, isn't this sweet? My favorite people all together." Lane put a napkin in my lap and then did the same with Van, who'd been seated to his right. "It's like a little reunion."

"Lane took a leave of absence to deal with some family stuff. This is his first semester back as he works on his MBA," Logan offered. "He was Alpha before Macen."

"Thank fuck he showed up. Being Alpha with this bunch of bitches and dumb ass pussy betas is a pain in the ass." Lane shoveled a few forkfuls of egg into his mouth. "So, Riles. I hear you had your first experience at Temple last night. Freaky shit, right?"

"You could say that." I chewed on my toast, the déjà vu almost knocking me out of my seat. "Thank you all again for your kindness yesterday. I'd left my appreciation with Stacy earlier since she's Macen's Alpha female."

Logan choked on his bacon for a few seconds. Lane chuckled beside me. The people around Stacy shifted uncomfortably. She glared at the two of them.

"Do you have something to say?" she demanded.

"Not at all. I think we'll leave that to Macen when he arrives." Logan winked. "And here I thought sleeping in would be fun."

"It sounds like we missed a hell of a conversation earlier," Lane said. "Anyone care to share?"

Mimes made more noise than the people at the table did. I shifted between the two guys and cleared my throat. "There's really nothing to share. They were kind enough to impart some pack culture."

"Oh, really? We have culture to impart? Do tell." Lane leaned back in his seat.

I could feel the people at the table stop breathing.

"Really, it's not worth mentioning. I'm truly thankful to understand things better now. It'll make my university experience much simpler."

"How so?" Logan asked.

I didn't want to air this before the two men. They were Macen's friends, his fellow pack mates. Shame rose in me as heat engulfed my cheeks. Did they know about the crypt last night?

They had to if Stacy did.

"I'd rather not discuss this."

"Very well," Lane replied. He cut a wedge of pancake off and shoved it into his mouth. Chewing for a few, he swallowed. "We'll discuss it when Macen arrives."

Stacy growled. "He has more important things to deal with than this freak. It's an insult she's even here. She isn't pack."

"Get that tone around me again, bitch wolf, and you won't be pack, either." Lane slammed his coffee down. "Unless you want your next meal coming from a straw, I'd advise you all to sit here like the cute, meek, and *silent* little pack we wish for every night."

"Told you those wet dreams of yours would disappoint," Logan commented. "Now, where were we? Oh, yes. What is this culture you have learned?"

"An Alpha's duty is to his pack. Any extension of that protection and care to an outside person is a gift—one which shouldn't be taken advantage of long term. I believe that summarizes my lesson quite succinctly."

"Unsuccinct it for us, babe," Lane leaned in to whisper in my ear. "A couple of the bitches across the table need shit dumbed down. Think of it like a mama bird chewing food, then puking it back up to feed them. You can do it."

"That's disgusting," Van said as she pushed her tray away.

No kidding. I swallowed the bile in my throat and accepted the grim reality I wasn't getting out of here without exposing my shame to the table yet again. Embarrassment crept within me.

"I am merely a project—a charity case, if you will. Macen is a kind Alpha who also cares for and protects needy, defective people like me. What happened at Temple and the crypt was him feeling sorry for me. I shouldn't expect it to happen again."

There. I'd ripped the bandage off. I could ignore the burning pain and the itching shame pulsating within me. I inhaled the tension in the air as the two men beside me dropped their forks.

"At least we know where you skulked off to last night. You followed them. That's pathetic, Stacy, even for you," Logan said.

Footsteps thudded up the stairs and my *oh shit* meter went nuclear red. Macen squeezed my shoulders. His voice was low and growly like liquid velvet across my skin. "Do you believe that shit, Riles?"

I didn't want to, but the truth settled in my belly like a heavy, scratchy monster. I was nothing to him. We'd just met yesterday. He pitied me.

I swallowed my tears and bowed my head as far as I could, hoping the guys beside me couldn't see the tears dropping from my eyes.

"Out." The booming order came from behind me, a malevolent rage which rumbled through me.

This wasn't good. I wanted invisibility, the anonymity I was accustomed to. Taking a deep breath, I focused on trying to handle the situation, the man before me. "Macen, please. You have better things to deal with. We'll talk about this later."

I heard people racing down the stairs. The seats beside me scraped along the floor when the guys stood.

"We'll sentry at the bottom." Lane and Logan headed down.

My heart beat wildly when I was lifted from my chair and set on the table. I didn't want to look at him, was terrified of what I'd see. Yet a part of me needed the contact, the awareness to finally sink in.

I was drowning in my fear of what last night meant. Had it meant nothing? Did I deserve for it to be anything beyond a good time?

Chapter Five

Macen

What the fuck?

If I didn't know better, I'd swear Riles was trying to piss me off with over-the-top melodramatic bullshit, which was more Stacy's style. No telling what the bitch had said to unravel the bonding thread Riles and I had woven last night.

I'd spent most of the morning dealing with drama because someone had called in a complaint about me offering Riles a place in our wolf pack. *My* fucking wolf pack.

It may be a shit campus in the middle of nowhere, but every wolf here was mine to handle and take care of. I took pride in being a decent Alpha for them. The call pissed me the fuck off.

And now this.

I couldn't handle chicks crying. My dad would've knocked Riles upside the head and told her to calm the fuck down. I'd be fucking damned if I was my old man.

"You're killing me, sweetheart." I drew her into my embrace, ignoring the tension in her shoulders and the way she held her arms between us, protectively covering her face.

Her shoulders shook as she silently broke down. Mother fucker.

I wanted to charge down the stairs and shake Stacy until I knew what I was dealing with, but I'd heard enough to establish the terrain. That bitch was predictable if nothing else.

I took a chance the sweet submissive little minx I'd had on my Harley the night before was there, buried beneath the layers of bullshit she'd been fed this morning. Tugging on her head firmly, I growled in her ear, low and long, until I felt the tension flow from her.

She shivered within my embrace, her arms falling between us. Blood surged to my cock. "You with me again, Riles?"

"Yes."

"I don't want you to speak. We clear?" When I felt her nod, I sighed into her ear, and let a few moments pass. Holding her made me want to spread her out on this table and feast on her.

"I don't give a shit what you heard or what went down here. All you need to know is *I* want you. I want you so fucking bad, Riles, all I can think about is stripping you bare and burying my dick in you so hard and deep you feel me in your throat. I'm a dominant son of a bitch, but you bring out a part of me I haven't unleashed. Ever."

Her pulse quickened beneath my lips. Her breathing became ragged against my ear. My dick hardened, and I couldn't help but pull forward on her ass until my hard length rubbed between her legs.

"Fucking Christ, I want to fuck you hard and long right here, so my whole pack hears you howl my name. I want this sweet pussy of yours seizing and gripping my dick when we come."

She fisted my shirt and gasped softly as her hips bucked against me.

"Is your sweet pussy wet for me, Riles?"

"Yes."

Fuck it. "Lean back and brace your hands above your head on the edge of the table."

"W-why?" She obeyed even as she questioned me. I didn't deserve her complete trust, but she gave it to me anyway.

I wanted to carry her to my room, but we'd never make it there. I wanted to bury myself deep in her, but she deserved better than a roll on a cafeteria table.

I wasn't about to let my girl roam around campus this needy. Hell no.

I unzipped her pants and gently drew the denim material and her little white panties down from her hips. I loved the fullness there; she'd feel good beneath me when we were in the depths of passion.

"Macen, we can't."

I leaned down and brushed my lips across hers, licking until she opened her mouth. She was sweeter than I'd remembered and so responsive my wolf surfaced, rumbling just beneath my skin.

He wanted to claim her, bite and mark her until everyone accepted she was mine. He was the most brilliant mother fucker around, but she deserved better than a quick romp on a cafeteria table.

My wolf would have to wait for his happy ending.

Right now was about Riles.

She relaxed beneath me. Her skin was warm when I explored beneath her top, pausing long enough to pay homage to those gorgeous tits. They spilled over my palms. Fuck, I loved curvy women.

She swallowed my growl with a hungry kiss that made my dick swell in my pants. I ground against her, grabbing her hips until she stilled. I'd forgotten she was bare below the waist until her wet heat coated my fingers.

I severed the kiss, licking and nibbling a path down

her body until my mouth was there. Her ache for me matched mine for her. A small gasp escaped her as I spread her folds and licked.

Her fingers wound in my hair. The dominant in me wanted to put them back, but I liked the way she clawed at me, pressing until my tongue was buried in her wet heat. I rubbed her clit until she was writhing.

I'd never get enough of my Riles.

Mine.

My wolf remained within striking distance as I licked and nipped her to the edge of release. Not burying my dick in her was the hardest thing I'd ever done, but I wanted her to know she was more than a quick romp.

Words were shit compared to proof. I intended to spend every waking moment proving that to her. I wanted her release on my tongue, in my mouth, so I could taste her all day. Her soft, panting moans had grown more intense. Louder.

I growled and rose to claim her mouth. Her eyes flew open, no doubt because she was startled to taste herself. The act was raunchy and the sexiest fucking kiss I'd ever shared. She worked her body against my hand, her clit striking my thumb with each movement.

Our gazes locked, and I swallowed her cries of release as though they were my own. Her arms wrapped around me as I deepened the kiss until we were both gasping for air.

If dudes were supposed to be cool about sex afterward, I was about to turn in my man card because that was the hottest thing I'd done. I grimaced when I realized I was still possessively gripping her hair.

I rose, releasing her completely. "You okay?"

"Y-Yeah." She smiled at me, a sexy pink appearing on her cheeks. Cuter than hell. "You?"

"I'll live." That was still being decided. I could break boards with my dick because it was so hard, but she didn't need to know that. I basked in her innocent smile.

I was king of the fucking world right now.

She straightened her clothing and cleared her throat nervously. "Wow. That was unexpected."

"Riles." I cupped her face and waited for her gaze to dart to mine. "I won't apologize for what we just did. Like I said, I'm not a good man. The next time we're alone, I'm going to have you. All of you."

She nodded.

"Now I'm going to have Van take you back to Ruger unless you have somewhere else you need to be. You ready for your first day tomorrow? You got enough supplies and stuff?"

She didn't have shit. I'd seen the pathetic suitcase the fucker had left her with. I'd seen the thirty bucks and change.

"I'll be fine."

"Van will help you pull some stuff from our stock. We've got truckloads of shit which never gets used because families keep donating it to our hall for their kids."

"I couldn't possibly impose."

"I'm only saying this once, sweetheart. You're mine, which means you're pack as far as I'm concerned, and I don't give a rat's ass what anyone says. I take care of my own."

She nodded.

I hated leaving her alone. Spending the day with her would go a long way to taming my wolf, but shit was hitting the fan in a big way, and I didn't want her to know I was neck deep in it because of her.

We made our way downstairs. Van waved from across the room. I kissed Riles on the forehead. Hopefully, Van would behave and be a good ally for her. I'd have to set Stacy's shit from today straight at some point, but I didn't have time for childish drama right now.

I didn't know Riles was on the menu this morning, or I would've placed my order.

I shoved Lane against the wall and allowed my wolf to lurch forward in my voice. "Touch her, and you die."

Well, that went well. Logan headed toward the door. *I told your dumb ass to stay out of it.*

That's the table I eat on, Lane grumbled.

Please. You got more pussy up there than most humans get their whole lives. Don't pull the grossed out bullshit with me. I wasn't in the mood.

"So, what now?" Logan asked when we got outside.

"We find out what ROAR has learned."

"Sort of early, isn't it? They haven't even had a full day."

"Can't handle her being there for long, man."

"I heard about the challenge," Lane stated.

"Fuck the challenge. Fuck Diego. This isn't about him. I want her in my hall. In my bed."

"Let's get to it, then," Logan said.

We made our way to the restricted portion of Wolf Hall. Taking a few moments before I reamed Stacy would be smart, but I came from a long line of hotheads, and I was about to channel every last one of those dead motherfuckers.

The office was an archaic throwback to a different era—one where packs trembled before their Alphas, and female Alphas would never pull half the shit Stacy had. I was all for women's liberation and empowering the pack, but I was envious of the dude whose picture stared at me from the wall.

Elias Cumberland. The first Alpha Wolf Hall leader over one hundred years ago. I stared at the picture a few moments, wondering what I should do about this cluster fuck. While I wanted to rip into Stacy, I recognized her role within the pack. This whole situation was a prime example of why these so-called university packs were screwed up.

She was supposed to be the Alpha female simply because she was voted in. Translation? My wolf was supposed to fully embrace her as my partner in all ways because she steamrolled herself over everyone three years ago when we were a bunch of strangers who made unilateral decisions with four-year repercussions.

Totally fucked up.

I sensed Logan and Lane behind me before a cloud of vanilla stench engulfed me. My body recoiled as warmth settled at my back and hands wrapped around my waist. Stacy pawed at me, running her hands across my chest and down my stomach southward to the remnants of my encounter with Riles.

"Don't touch me." The feral growl drew her back, and for once, I was thankful for my wolf's bluntness.

I turned, allowing my rage to loom between us in a thick wave of disgust. She was a lot of things—a maniacal, self-absorbed bitch most days—but she wasn't stupid.

"I don't understand all these pathetic little causes you take up, Macen. Really. You have more than enough to handle with this pack, not to mention your family's issues."

"Don't mention my family again."

"I'm supposed to be your lead female. It's my duty to help, listen to your problems." She approached, resting her hand on my chest. "To do whatever you need me to."

"What I need is for you to stay the hell out of my business and back the hell off Riles."

"She's not pack." Anger flared within her gaze when she stepped away.

"Back off."

"You can't control what I do with freaks like her. She's. Not. Pack."

I grabbed her hair and flipped her around, bending her

over the desk. My wolf snarled and nipped beneath the surface when her wolf surfaced in her moan. "This is what you want, isn't it? You want me to bend you over, strip you down, and mount you right here in front of Logan and Lane. You probably want them to join in."

Her ass rubbed against my limp dick. Jesus, I couldn't stand this bitch.

I waited until she stilled beneath me. "If you do anything to her, or have any of your little pack go near her, I will make sure none of this pack will ever fuck you again. We clear?"

"You can't do that."

"Watch me." I shoved her away from me. "Get the hell out of here."

"That was entertaining." Lane smirked as he and Logan approached.

"I feel for the Alpha who lands with her."

"She needs a firm hand and a few lessons." Logan shrugged. "She's bangable."

"I'll keep that in mind and send her your way next time she comes sniffing around." I sat at the desk and leaned back in the chair. So much for a quiet Saturday morning. "What've we got on the agenda today?"

"I went through the messages while you were dealing with Stacy. ROAR left a message, and someone from your father's house called, but there wasn't a message."

"Great."

"He pressuring you to take over?"

"Yeah. Shit's hitting the fan with a couple of the neighboring packs, and he doesn't want to deal with it any longer. Since one of those packs is Stacy's, he figures I need to deal with it since I cock blocked his grand plan of uniting our packs through a mating."

"That probably didn't settle well with either of the old men if they're anything like mine. That generation is all into tradition and shit." Lane sighed. "Sucks to be you, man."

Ignoring his comment, I pressed the speaker of the phone beside me and dialed the ROAR hotline. I hadn't expected answers to my questions this quickly, but they always amazed me.

"Macen, it's always a pleasure."

I laughed. "Somehow I doubt that, but you are very kind to say so. I hope you have good news for me."

"I'm afraid we've hit a few roadblocks. The blood test results were somewhat anomalous, so the lab is rerunning with a new sample. I've also contacted the Paranormal Enforcement Agency for their input into the situation in reference to the dean's placement of her within Demonia-controlled land. I'm afraid our hands are tied until I hear back from them."

"I was hoping we could resolve the situation locally."

"Me, too, but the school board doesn't want to go on the record with this one, Macen. The precedent could prove very detrimental to the university in the future. From what I can tell, the pack she was with is quite influential—deep pockets."

"Not in the mood to play university politics on this one. Help me out here."

"We're working on it. Until then, the university is increasing patrols around Ruger Hall and setting up welfare checks for Riletta."

"Our moves might make things uncomfortable for her at Ruger. I don't want her dealing with the backlash. I don't want her scared. What's the big deal about her residing here at Wolf Hall for the interim?"

"Prince Drecor has assured me no harm will come to her."

"That doesn't mean shit since the prince is never there to rein in his hellhounds."

Lane and Logan nodded their heads, their grim expressions matching my mood. Time was running out, and this discussion had me remembering what was to go down Friday night. One way or the other this shit had to get sorted.

Call waiting beeped. I sighed. "Gotta go, another call. Thanks for the help."

"We'll get this handled, Macen. Don't worry."

I clicked over to the other call with a growl of frustration when I saw the caller ID register my father. "Yes?"

"Mace." The sniffled reply was barely audible.

I leaned forward, too aware of my thudding heart and held breath. Clarissa never called me. "Hey, sis. What's wrong?"

"You need to come home. M-Mom and Dad...they...." She gasped weepy air and sniffled. "Mace, they're dead."

Chapter Six

Riles

Some evil bastard was trying to kill me. It was the only explanation I had for the Sahara-worthy dryness of my mouth and the incessant sledgehammer battering my brain into mush. Nausea kept me still as I blinked the room into focus. Thank God Vira hated the sun. If just one ray hit me right now, I'd probably die.

Why the hell had I bothered to survive last night? Maybe I didn't. Every muscle in my body ached, and I was pretty sure the shirt I had on wasn't mine. Or Vira's.

"Finally. I was starting to think you weren't gonna make it." Vira stood over me with an amused smirk. "Get a move on. Group starts in fifteen."

Group. I tried to think but winced as the pain in my temples increased. Okay, I didn't need to understand her. Obedient minions never require a brain. A groan escaped me, and I tumbled out of bed. Pain shot through my knees; my stomach roiled.

"You puke near my bed, I'll make you lick it up." *Gross.* The threat made the rumbling worse. Vira grabbed my arm and hauled me into the bathroom, slamming me into a worshipping position in front of the toilet. "Next time, you listen to me, princess. Lemon drops are not your friend."

I wasn't drinking ever again. Memories of shot after shot as I valiantly defended my blatant stupidity in a fucked-up game called "Around the World" assailed me. I'd stood no chance since the focal point of the game was Demonia. What the hell had I been thinking?

"Lookit, you got street cred with the newbies around here for trying to fit in, but your ass is on the radar with the upper classmen. That's fucked up, princess." Vira turned on the water as I purged my gut. She sighed and yanked my hair back with a bit more force than necessary. "I get your need to fit in, but it ain't ever happening. The sooner you sort that shit in your head, the happier I'll be. And you want me happy. Trust me. A pissed Vira is never good."

I suspected any Vira was never a good thing, but silence was golden in this situation. Someone had shoved a year's supply of cotton balls down my throat. Vira secured my hair in a loose pony tail at the base of my neck.

"Here. Drink." She yanked my head up. The gruff tone brooked no argument. I watched her as I gulped water from the glass she held. When the contents were gone, she stepped back. "You'll live."

As I waited for the imminent round two of nausea, I realized my life had changed somewhat dramatically the past couple of days—most of which was thanks to Vira. She'd taken me on as a pet project because she "didn't trust any mangy, wet mutts to do things right." The mutts in question were Macen and the other wolves. I wouldn't be sharing her thoughts with them anytime soon.

"Why are you doing this?" When she glared back at me, I clarified. "Helping me."

"I always wanted a pain in the ass little sister. I figure you're as close as I'll get. Don't worry. I'll make it worth my while in the long run. I always do."

She'd make a good big sister. I envied her kick-butt persona more each day. I'd been working on channeling my inner Riles, that courageous spitfire Macen seemed to think lurked beneath the surface. Being around Vira made finding that part of me simpler, almost instinctive at times.

She was freaking awesome, but I wouldn't share that with her. She wouldn't want me to. My gratitude would remain unspoken because that was the way cool people like Vira did shit. It was one of the many things I'd learned over the past few days, thanks to my new adaptive process. Watch. Listen. Learn.

"Change. We'll grab a coffee and muffin at the coffee shop on the way to group. They don't like people being late to that shit, so make sure you're on time." She flung a pile of clothes at me and left the bathroom.

Okay, apparently I was going to group—whatever the heck that was. A few minutes later, I was tooth brushed, spit polished, properly deodorized, and somewhat clothed. I resembled something the hellhounds had dragged in from the gutter, but I was mobile and shoed in sneakers the moment I left the bathroom.

Vira sneered at my footwear a few moments. Clearly, bargain bin tennies were a faux pas for a shoe fiend like her. Her closet groaned under the weight of her designer fetish. I settled my gaze on today's stilettos of choice—red leather flames that seemed to lick her ankles. Cute. So her.

Totally kick ass.

A backpack landed in my arms. She tugged me into the hallway and slammed our door shut. "You aren't a morning person."

"I'm pretty sure I'm not a person at all today."

"You'll get used to it. The first hangover's always the worst, and those lemon drops are potent. They use Demonia liquor, which is like two hundred proof."

"Good to know *after* the fact."

"Told you that shit last night, princess. You just didn't want to hear me." Vira chuckled. "I bet you will next time."

"There won't be a next time." I cringed when we exited the building. The sun's rays battered my eyeballs. "Oh, geez."

"Here, use these."

I snatched up the sunglasses Vira offered with swift gratitude, which seemed to make her more amused. Yeah, I was pretty damn pathetic this morning. Fortunately, the line at the small Demonia coffee shop was nonexistent— probably because all of them were smart enough to still be passed out in the dorm.

She handed me a large coffee and a muffin of questionable origin. I didn't want to know what made this coffee shop different from any of the other "normal" ones. Sometimes not knowing was the best route, and I was relatively certain I would be paving that bitch highway as my own by the time Vira was done mentoring me.

"Now that you're awake, gotta say a couple of things while we're outside of Ruger. We keep this shit between ourselves until we come up with a plan of action. Feel me?"

I nodded like a good pupil as we made our way to wherever we were going at a rigorous pace. The list of questions I had for her was growing, but I figured I'd keep adding on until she seemed to be in the mood to handle my naivety. Today wasn't that day.

I wasn't sure that day would ever exist, but whatever. One thing I'd learned long ago was that it was sometimes easier to stumble around and figure stuff out on your own. You could stay under the radar that way.

"Last night, you fell and cut your arm on a glass table. I got to you first, patched you up." Vira halted and waited until I was staring directly at her. "Your blood burned me. It tasted like honey."

Wait. What? "You ate my blood?" *Ewww.*

Obviously, there were facets of our budding friendship I wasn't prepared for. My roomie chowing down on my blood like I was din-din was at the top of the list. I blinked a couple of times, assessing my ability to outrun her if the situation got anymore awkward. Of course, I had nowhere to run to, but I'd figure that out when the time came.

This was me—the new Riles. Sorting shit out as I went, not letting the fact I knew no one and had nothing get me down. I would look whatever the problem was straight in the face even if it was my blood-thieving roomie. "I'm sorry, what?"

"That shit pumping through your veins is serious, and I'm a little fucking pissed I've gotten dragged into it. Dealing with what it probably means puts a serious damper on my existence."

"What does it mean?" I ignored the whole discussion about her eating my blood. To hell with it. She'd digested my fracking blood. "And excuse the taste. It wasn't like I invited you to dine on me."

Freak.

She's half vampire, you idiot. Of course she's into blood.

A shudder escaped me as I glared at her. "Don't take my blood again."

Her eyes widened slightly, her lips upturned into an outright grin. "Damn. You do have a spine after all. This should be interesting. All I know is you are serious trouble—the kind we can't even talk about until I figure out what our options are."

"You're making no sense." I sighed my exhaustion as the sun battered my patience. Shifting the backpack to my other shoulder, Prickles of unease streamed along my spine. "Do you know what I am?"

"You know who my dad is, right?"

I nodded. He was some head honcho for the Vampire

King—aka Vira's first cousin, or something like that. He was the main reason everyone gave her a wide berth. He was more than a little protective of his only child.

"Well, Pops has been around for quite a while and been just about everywhere as ambassador. So have I." She sighed heavily and looked around. When she saw no one around us, she continued, her voice lowered. "There are a lot of legends about the way things used to be. Centuries ago, there was another dimension that oversaw this world and Demonia. Two factions of beings existed there—angels and phoenixes. I need to talk to Pops, but I think you might be part one of those things. Your blood isn't right. I've tasted just about everything in existence, and you're different."

All righty, then. Unsure what to do with that huge dump of what-the-frack, I nodded. "Interesting."

"You don't get it. Creatures from that dimension are the only things capable of easily killing any other species in existence. They could destroy entire factions with a mere thought."

Wow. I so wasn't that.

"I see that look. You don't believe me. You don't need to. All you need to do is keep your mouth shut about this and not let anyone mess with your blood in any way. Once I hear from Pops, we'll figure it out. Okay?"

"Okay, but ROAR already has my blood."

"That's okay. They're probably the only ones we could trust right now. Besides, it'll take weeks for them to move on anything. It's the start of the school year, and they're probably overrun with issues." Vira continued walking. "Don't worry. We'll figure it out. In the meantime, you can check out the legends and folklore section of the library. There's lots of info on that world in the Demonia section on the top floor."

The library. The missing puzzle pieces tumbled into place. Group study for Business Math. Vira had arranged for me to sit in with some of the first year demons, vampires, and hellhounds. Apparently, Demonians were killer math whizzes.

"You know, I'm not sure they'll let me into the library. They didn't let me past the receptionist's desk last time I tried." I'd been desperate for a computer. Apparently, reports and papers were supposed to be typed, not scrawled on notebook paper.

"We'll get you sorted."

I breathed a sigh of relief. That was always Vira's response, and somehow, like Macen, she always managed to sort it out. The brief thought of Macen filled me with nervousness. I hadn't heard from him since....

My face heated. My pulse raced.

"Don't. I told you not to think about him when we're out," she growled. "They can smell your arousal."

I swallowed and looked around, thankful few people were milling around outside the massive library as we made our way up the steps. Unease made my steps falter. The shrill woman behind the desk had been quite rude the last time I'd tried to enter. Then again, she'd been nice the other three times before that.

I pressed closer to Vira when she paused to wait for me. Maybe I could slide in behind her, and they wouldn't say anything. Over the past couple of days, I'd figured out very few people said much to her. She was as much an outsider in the Demonia sector of the campus as I was in the shifter sector. That's probably why I wanted so badly to be more like her, adapt myself to her style of handling situations.

The turn-style door crunched us closer. My pulse flailed as I tried to take a few deep breaths to calm the anxiousness now bursting within me. I hated confrontation more than anything.

"Hey." She turned and squeezed my arm the moment we exited the claustrophobic nightmare of a doorway.

"I've got your back, Riles. No matter what shit I may give you, we're tight now. Okay?"

I nodded. My rattled nerves settled. I wasn't alone anymore. I had a friend. I had more than one friend if I counted Macen. "Thanks."

"Let's do this." Vira walked to the desk, and I inwardly winced when the shrill woman's narrowed gaze landed on me like lasers from a sighted weapon.

"Miss Riletta, while I admire your tenacity, I'm contacting campus security. Perhaps the dean could get you to understand you are not welcome in this building until you have the proper identification." She picked up a phone.

"Seriously?" Vira asked. "It's a library. What's she going to do? Research you to death?"

The woman's mouth pursed as she honed her beamed gaze on Vira. "I fail to see how this is your concern, Miss Aradi. Perhaps you should leave security measures to me and head to your floor. I believe many of your kind arrived a while ago."

"Well, my kind can wait until I have my girl sorted. Now, what identification is it that you require for her to walk into a building my father paid for? Perhaps I should have him discuss these security measures you are undertaking with the University Board. We wouldn't want to tax you with such a high level of responsibility." She pulled her phone out and started pushing buttons.

The woman lunged toward Vira, her upper half leaning over the counter. "That won't be necessary, Miss Aradi. I'm sure we can handle this one situation amongst ourselves, given the circumstances. It is a shame to make Riletta wait for all the red tape on her identifications. And, like you said, it's just a library card, right?"

Vira pocketed her phone and flicked an impatient gaze across her nemesis. "Certainly. Perhaps for future reference, you will recall this situation and handle other students in this predicament with a bit more care. And, by the way, her name is Riles, not Riletta. There's a huge pack of wolves that'll get pretty irked if they see that name on her card, and, believe me, those meddling mutts know everything when it comes to her."

The woman blanched. Her fingers trembled as she tapped the keyboard. "Of course, I wasn't aware she was affiliated with them. What last name am I using?"

I'd mentioned, the first couple of visits, that I was at Ruger Hall, but would more than likely be relocated to Wolf Hall soon. "I don't have a last name."

"Use Giordano. We might as well cut through the bullshit and call it like it is."

The woman's eyes widened. "Oh, my. Well, okay, then. Giordano, it is. Once again, my sincerest apologies, Miss Giordano."

Vira smirked, and I couldn't help but suspect I was missing something important. I'd never heard that name before, had no idea where she would've come up with it. Hopefully, it wouldn't cause problems for me down the road.

I stood on the duct-taped X on the floor and smiled into the camera when told to. Moments later, I was the proud owner of my first identification card. And, Jesus, I looked worse than I had imagined.

"Ha! See? Every I.D. card picture is horrible even for gorgeous things like you." Vira headed toward the elevator. "Don't lose that. Until you get your other cards, that's as good as gold around here to prove who you are and what faction you're affiliated with."

I studied the card and noted the wolf's head in the corner of the card. She'd affiliated me with Macen's pack. "I hope he doesn't mind me referencing his pack."

"I'm thinking that'll be the last thing he notices if he ever gets ahold of your card." Vira chuckled. "Let's go get you math savvy."

Hopefully, afterward, I could stay up there and look into the whole angel and phoenix thing. I doubted Vira knew what she was talking about. It made no sense for me to be something that rare since I was as ordinary as possible.

"I can't wait to show Macen this card. I finally have an I.D."

"I can't wait for you to show him either."

Chapter Seven

Riles

I'd morphed into a new person in a matter of a few days. The freedom worked wonders on my self-esteem. I loved my classes except for Business Math, but, really, who loved math? I smiled inwardly as I settled into my new hidey hole—a table on the top story of the library.

No one ever came up here. It was the perfect spot. I'd grown accustomed to having a hidey hole a few months into my second year with Jacob's pack when I realized no one liked me. Until then, I'd been relatively sheltered within Elise's care.

My fifth birthday party had changed everything. That was when the entire pack had finally realized how freakish I was. I couldn't shift. All the other kids had shifted, running and chasing one another in wolf form. There I was, scampering along with my weak human legs, totally unaware I was an abomination from that point forward.

Every child shifted by age five.

I was defective, tossed to the outskirts of the city where pack members serving out punishments took shifts attending to my need for food and clean clothes when they remembered. A few saw to my education, so I wouldn't reflect badly on Jacob if anyone ever learned I was raised by them.

I cast away the negative emotions brought on by the past and pulled out my purple binder, which matched my purple backpack. The supplies I'd ferreted from Wolf Hall were beyond cool. I'd wanted to thank Macen myself, but I hadn't seen him since....

Heat rose in my face when I remembered what we'd done Saturday. Four days had passed since then, but my body still heated at the memory and the words that'd settled into my fantasies.

The next time we're alone, I'm going to have you.

I hadn't expected to wait this long, but I could only imagine how hectic things had been for him. I'd barely managed to stay afloat, and I didn't have a huge pack to tend to on top of senior level courses.

He hadn't called.

Insecurities had crushed me a few times. I'd passed Wolf Hall several times the last couple of days and seen Stacy and her crew lurking around outside. I'd hoped to see Van, maybe Logan or Lane. I wanted to make sure Macen was okay. It didn't mean I was obsessed with him or anything.

You're only repaying his kindness. He worried about you. It makes sense you'd do the same in return. It means nothing more.

Sure. I kept telling myself this again and again because the alternative was too terrifying. I couldn't have gotten melded to him that quickly. I'd heard of it happening with heart mates, but I wasn't wolf. Or even a shifter.

He'd never be mine.

Hopefully, he wasn't avoiding me. It wasn't like I had expectations.

"Riletta."

I jumped when I heard the terse voice boom behind

me. "Hi, Dean Sandusky."

"Come with me."

"What's going on?"

The dean sighed and pulled out his cellphone. "Why does everything have to be a challenge with you?"

I tensed, his disdain echoing Jacob's. I'd been away from his grasp for almost a week and had just acclimated to not feeling the tension, the angst of waiting for the next insult or chastisement.

"I'm sorry you think so, Dean. I would merely like to know where I'm going and why. Safety first, you know." I shoved my binder back into my backpack and looked at him as I stood. "Is there a problem?"

"With you, there's always a problem." He grasped my arm with his meaty hand and pulled me toward the stairwell.

I wanted to punch and shove him away, but my pulse quickened as my mind processed his size versus mine. He was too big, and I was alone. Maybe this hidey hole wasn't the best after all.

How had he found me up here?

I grimaced under the pressure of his fingers digging into my flesh, but remained silent as he dragged me toward what I assumed was his office on the top floor of the building beside the library. I surmised he must've seen me enter from his lofty perch.

Asshole.

He shoved me into a chair and sat behind his desk with a smug grin on his face. He reminded me of a peacock minus the feathers, strutting around as though everyone wanted to be him.

"Is there a problem, sir?"

"Your test results came back inconclusive." He shoved the paper toward me.

"Okay."

What was I supposed to say? I'd known that would

happen.

"I understand from Prince Drecor your presence within Ruger is causing problems. Apparently you have ROAR agitated about your situation, and it's causing security concerns for him."

"I'm afraid I can't help you, sir. I contacted ROAR and asked a few questions, but I never complained about my living situation or the residents of Ruger Hall. I'm not sure where the Prince is getting his information from, but I can assure you I'm not trying to create problems."

"Well, you need to call off your mutt if you want to remain here. I can't tolerate dissension within this university. I warned Jacob I wouldn't tolerate nonsense from you. However, because I do respect him, I'll give you until the end of the day to get Macen to withdraw his complaints with the university." He glared at me from over the top of his black-rimmed glasses. "This is hardly ROAR's concern since we have yet to even establish what you are. I doubt you fall within their jurisdiction."

The problem was I fell nowhere.

"I'll see to it, sir. Is there anything else?" I perched myself on the edge of my chair, ready to spring out of the room.

My skin crawled when I was near him. At least he'd given me a plausible excuse to leave. I had to speak with Macen immediately. I couldn't afford to get kicked out of this school since Jacob had made it quite clear I was never to return to the Cervantez pack.

"That will be all." He glared up at me when I stood. "I'll expect a *very* profound apology from you to the Prince for the trouble you caused. He was kind enough to give you accommodations, and you returned his kindness with theatrics. You are not in jeopardy, Riletta. No one cares whether you live or die, so why should anyone give a damn if you are here or not? This isn't about you. This is about ensuring the students of this university are not adversely impacted by your presence."

I coughed to avoid sniffling as I responded to his words. I hated that I still had a soft underbelly, the one men like him exposed and pounded on with ruthless efficiency. I should be immune to the whip of hatred by now, but it still stung as badly as it had the first time.

"I don't want to cause problems, sir. I merely want to study like everyone else and live without worry."

"Well, Riletta, it's time you accept you are an abomination. Your very existence undermines all the diplomatic work we've done for nearly a century to get paranormal beings on an equal footing with humans. The fact you are none of the things we've proven are safe and willing to abide by the Code of Conduct is an insult to everything we've strived for."

I kept my gaze downward, but I sensed the smugness in his voice. He'd shattered the bubble of contentment I'd constructed the past few days. Jacob would be proud of him.

"Leave before I decide not to be so lenient and kick your ass off this university right now."

I fled the room, swiping at my face as I raced down the stairwell. I had to stop this. I had to figure out a way to exist here without a problem.

All I'd wanted was an identity, papers to work. Make my own way. Alone.

I could handle it. I'd done well enough so far.

Wolf Hall was across campus, which I was thankful for. It gave me enough time to get myself pulled together and somewhat prepared for Stacy. There'd be a run-in. The fact I'd avoided it all week was a small miracle.

I took the steps up to the visitor's entrance, my stomach roiling, my heart heavy. I didn't want to do this. I wanted to know what I was. I didn't want to be in Ruger Hall.

I wanted the normalcy Macen dangled before me.

"I'd hoped you had enough sense not to come around here." Stacy pranced to stand in front of me the moment I stepped into Wolf Hall. A cluster of women and a couple of men stood around her, snarling. It was almost comical to imagine a pack as ferocious and massive as this one being so obsessed with hating a nothing like me.

"I need to speak with Macen."

"I tried to warn you, but you didn't listen. If he hasn't called or seen you, he's not interested. Get lost." Stacy shoved me. Her blonde hair swished around her shoulders as she advanced on me. "I'm done being nice. He's got too much shit on his plate to deal with your pathetic ass."

Anger kept me standing there even though I wanted to flee, to forget I'd ever stumbled across Macen and this pack. I didn't need this shit from her.

"I'm not leaving until I talk to him."

"You're in for a long wait. He's not here," a guy behind Stacy stated. "His pack back home needed him."

"Is he okay?"

"That's not your business, bitch." Stacy shoved me again.

"Leave her be."

Lane made his way down the massive staircase. Crap on a swizzle stick. I didn't want to deal with this man. He was too big, too everything. He terrified me on a primal level.

Like Macen without the softness.

The clustering pack dispersed quickly, leaving Stacy alone in the stare down she'd started with me. I wasn't leaving until I knew he was okay. I'd figure out some other way to deal with my issues.

Maybe I could call ROAR myself and speak with them. Surely, I had a right to stop whatever they were doing if it had to do with me. Right?

Lane loomed in front of me, having shoved Stacy out of the way without my notice. I stopped my memorization of the floor and looked up. And up. Jesus, he was too freaking tall. I studied the floor again.

Warm fingers caressed my chin and pulled softly until I stared into his obsidian gaze. A smile appeared on his face as I swallowed. Even though he was gorgeous, my body didn't sing for him like it did with Macen. Heat coursed through me when I thought about him.

"Is Macen okay?"

"I just spoke with him. He had to leave for a family emergency Saturday right after we left you. My apologies for not telling you."

"I didn't have any right to know. I actually came for a different reason. I'm sorry for being so nosy."

"Come." He wrapped an arm around my shoulders and led me to a small room off the entryway.

The door clicked closed behind us, and pangs of nervousness crawled across my skin. I didn't know what to expect from this stranger. Would he be like Jacob? Or more like Macen?

Tension kept me frozen, locked in the possible scenarios I ran through my mind. Having conversational exit strategies had worked well for me in the past.

"You done thinking everything through, or do you need a minute?" He flashed a grin when I looked at him. "You remind me of a girl in my pack back home—always thinking things through before she spoke, never wanted to make waves."

He was too astute.

"Thing was, she did that 'cause her pa was a piece of shit who needed to be taken out back and ripped into pieces. I've got to say, seeing her in you doesn't make my wolf happy."

"Sorry."

"Don't ever apologize for being, Riles. The sooner you learn that, the better things'll be." Lane leaned against the wall across from me, giving me enough space to breathe deeply and calm down.

"I was hoping Macen would be here and have a moment to speak with me. I swear it has nothing to do with…." What the hell was I thinking? I'd almost blurted out what we'd done Saturday. "I just need him to handle something for me."

"Well, I'm afraid he's not going to be around for the next few days, possibly longer. His parents were killed in a car accident."

No. My knees gave out. Something within me stirred, shifted into place. My vision speckled with white dots as I found myself held up by Lane.

"Whoa. What just happened?"

I don't know.

"Sit down." He settled me into a chair and knelt to look at me. "You get dizzy?"

"I think so."

Lane went to the corner behind the desk and grabbed water from the mini-fridge. "Here. Drink this. All of it."

Bossy Alpha.

He chuckled. "I saw that look. I think Macen hasn't figured out what a handful you really are."

Oh, he's had his hands full of me a time or two.

At Lane's burst of laughter, I cursed. "Did I just say that out loud?"

"I believe so."

"Sorry. I'm pretty sure Vira's been rubbing off on me the past few days."

"I'm not. I just wish Stacy had been here to hear it. Set that bitch in her place once and for all."

"That would be mean," I whispered. I sipped on my water for a moment and considered my options. "Please send my condolences to Macen when you speak with him. I can't imagine how hard this must be for him."

Actually, I could. In a way. I'd mourned my family my entire life. Then again, I hadn't ever known them, so I couldn't possibly ache as much as Macen did. I certainly had zero business unloading my problems at their doorstep right now.

"Thank you for helping." I stood to leave and found myself gently pushed back into the chair. He pulled out his phone and tendrils of unease rippled through me. "Please don't, Lane."

"Don't what?"

"Don't do whatever you're about to do because I know you shouldn't, whatever it is."

"Hey, man. Need a few to handle something here." He held the phone away from his ear and whistled at the roar of curse words streaming through the room. "Dial it down there, buddy."

I couldn't do this. My God, how selfish was I to even think to sit here and let him bother Macen with my melodrama? I'd figure something out, starting with an apology to Prince Drecor.

"Move, and I'll put you over my knee." Lane chuckled and winked. "I am Macen's stand-in after all."

Heat rose in my cheeks. My butt ached from the hard thud it had taken against the chair.

"Man, dial it back, or I'm not passing the phone." He chuckled some more. "Yeah. Yeah. Love ya, too, buddy."

My heartbeat thundered in my ears when I took the phone. What should I say? "Riles."

The pain and need in his voice was so evident, I stopped breathing. Tears clouded my vision. I'd give anything to make the hurt in his voice go away.

"I wish I could make it all go away," I whispered. I couldn't apologize. No amount of apology for his loss would make it go away. Nothing would, not even time. It simply dulled to a tolerable throb, a chasm in your soul which couldn't be filled.

"I wanted to call, but you don't have a phone, do you?"

"No."

"We'll be changing that."

There he was, the wolf in shining armor set on righting every wrong I'd been dealt. Something stirred deep in me once more. Calm coursed through my blood. I closed my eyes and inhaled deeply, wishing I was closer so I could hold him, kiss away the tears he'd never shed. I wanted to be his rock as he'd been mine, yet I knew I had no right.

"Are you the eldest?" He was too Alpha not to be.

"Yes." He cleared his throat, his voice thick with emotion. "Pops had begged me to come home, take over. I should've listened."

"That wouldn't have stopped an accident. This isn't your fault."

"Fuck, I needed to hear those sweet words from your sexy voice."

Lane averted his gaze, studying the wall as though it would come to life at any moment, seemingly unable to hear the sensual stream of need rumbling from the phone, heightening the angst I'd been carrying for days.

"I need you, babe. Need you to let me bury myself so deep in you I can't remember any of this bullshit."

I had no words. None. Need pulsed between my legs, hardened my nipples to throbbing buds. Simply thinking about him possessing me, commanding my body, made me ignite.

Lane raised his eyebrows and backed up a bit. He crossed his arms and studied me. Looking away, ashamed of my quick-fire reaction to Macen.

"How long will you be gone?"

"Longer than I want to be. A couple of weeks." He cleared his throat again. "No one told you?"

"No. I-I've been busy and haven't seen anyone." The half-truth hung between us.

"You been dodging the hall?"

"No, I walked by a few times."

"No one saw you?"

"I'm not pack. I didn't need to know where you were." I lowered my voice when I saw Lane's gaze narrow to small pinpoints of disagreement. "It was private."

"Nothing's private from you, Riles."

The sentiment made me warm. My skin prickled with awareness. "I wish you were here."

I whispered the confession, half ashamed Lane could hear and half terrified Macen would laugh. I didn't want to be one of those fawning women I used to hear the Alphas from our pack bitching about.

"Me too, babe. Me, too."

Oh. My. God. He wanted me with him. I breathed a few deep breaths, trying not to sound so damn giddy. And clingy. I didn't want to be the static cling in this relationship, if that's what it was.

I didn't know exactly what to think about all this. I definitely couldn't risk being clingy. "I'd better let you get back to your business."

"Not so quick, sweetheart. You going to tell me why you finally came by the hall?"

"It can wait. It wasn't important."

"Let me decide that."

That couldn't happen. The moment Macen got wind of what the dean had said, the threats he'd made, he would be pissed. There were other ways to handle my troubles without bugging him. It'd be good for me.

Empowering.

"Macen, you need to focus on your family and pack. They need you."

"And you don't?"

Yes. I need you more than I wish I did. I need your strength, your courage. "Everything's fine with me, Macen. If anything goes south, I'll search out Lane or Logan."

"You do that. I'll make sure they give you a phone and program everyone's numbers into it. And, Riles...."

"Yeah?"

"This weekend, you are mine. Pack a bag. One of the guys will bring you up here."

Wow. I should argue, politely refuse. He had enough to deal with. Babysitting a freak wasn't on the priority list.

But it was for him.

Elation made my brain stammer, shut down the self-recriminating thoughts that'd become second nature. I mattered to him. He wanted me there.

"Okay."

"I've heard your classes are going well."

"You've heard?"

"Of course. You didn't think I'd leave you there without someone watching your back, did you?" He sighed. "You're pack, Riles. You're mine."

"Vira's been showing me the ropes. I've learned a lot the past few days. She even got me a library card even though my identification paperwork hasn't gone through yet. Vira had them set me up as part of the Wolf pack. I hope that's okay."

"I wouldn't have it any other way."

I shivered in delight. God, I loved his voice. "I can't wait to see you."

"Me, either. You don't know how good it is to hear your voice. Shit here hasn't been good."

"Well, I'll be there soon, and I can help. Don't think you're going to coddle me while I'm there. The new Riles Giordano can handle shit much better. Vira's said so."

Lane sputtered and coughed as Macen grew silent.

"Macen? You there?"

"Yeah, baby, I'm here. I'm liking the new name a lot. Make sure to use it on your other paperwork, okay?"

"Okay, I will." I looked over at Lane, who was silently laughing. Tears tracked down his face. "I'd better go. I think something's wrong with Lane. He's acting funny."

"Put him on, and I'll see you soon."

Lane took the phone before I said anything more, proving what I'd already known—wolves heard everything. That was so inconvenient. And embarrassing. He smiled at me as he spoke with Macen. "Hey, what's up?"

He listened for a few minutes and cursed. "Man, get real. You have any idea how hard that'll be to keep a lid on?"

Hearing only one side of a conversation was annoying—especially since the other side was Macen. Was everything okay? I'd see him soon. Right now, I needed to focus on getting out of my predicament on my own. Vira had already done too much. I couldn't involve her and risk Prince Drecor getting upset with her for helping me.

"Fine. I'll handle it. Stay safe, and we'll see you soon." Lane clicked the phone off and tossed it onto the chair beside him. "I'm glad you came by, Riles. I should've made sure you two spoke earlier. You calm his wolf."

A thrill rushed through me. "I'm glad. He calms me."

"You need anything?"

If only it was that simple. Unfortunately, my problem couldn't involve Wolf Hall or Vira. For once, I was going to stand on my own two feet and sort my own shit. "I'm fine. Thanks."

He studied me for a moment and shook his head. "You lie for shit, little one. You want to try again?"

"Not particularly."

"Riles."

"Really, I'm fine. If things go too far sideways, I'll let you know."

Chapter Eight

Getting out of Wolf Hall was more difficult than getting in. Lane, in his infinite Alphaness, assigned a couple of guys to shadow me over to Ruger Hall. Apparently, I needed this.

His expression had grown grim. He'd grown silent and generally a pain in my ass once I hung up from Macen. After an hour, he finally released me into the trust of Growly Brent and Growlier Corbin. They were thick, massive brick walls of ruggedness that made awesome battering rams as we moved through the crush of students hovering in the quad area of campus. Since classes had dispersed for the day, the common area had become socialization central.

Once we made it to Ruger, I paused and flashed a smile of gratitude to my two shadows. I waited until they left to exhale my relief. For a moment, I'd been worried they'd keep following me, and I suspected the next hour or so would be quite uncomfortable.

If they had hung around, they'd try to fix the mess. That's what Alpha wolves did. This pack had way too many hot-headed men in my humble opinion.

I'd learned the lay of the land with Ruger Hall from Vira after I vowed never, ever to use said knowledge.

She'd grown on me—or rather I had grown on her—the past few days. She'd mellowed. Somewhat. And I'd grown a spine—not that it'd help me when she found out what I did.

Sorry, Vira. I gotta do this.

She was totally going to kick my ass for this.

Fortunately, it was early enough in the late afternoon for me to race up the first couple of flights of stairs without issue. The freshmen and sophomore demons still partied pretty hard, so for them, rising before nightfall was rare—if not downright impossible.

I got a couple of glares from the third level juniors, but they let me race down the hall in a frantic need to find the next stairwell. Bouts of laughter echoed behind me.

I didn't want to know what they found so amusing.

Ignorance was bliss.

Vira had warned me the top two stories were deadly for me. Seniors and upper level personnel with zero patience for non-demons resided there. Some were restricted to the hall because they were so violent.

I gulped a few puffs of air until I surrendered to the fact it wasn't going to help steady my nerves. They were frayed bundles of Oh-Shit-I'm-Really-Doing-This. I yanked the door open wide and bounded up the stairs two at a time.

Yes, I was a freshman pansy about to dive, desperation first, into the upper echelon of Ruger Hall. They'd just have to deal with my freakish existence in their airspace long enough for me to get to the last stairwell and make my way up to Prince Drecor.

Showing up on his floor without an appointment probably wasn't prudent, but desperate times and all that. He wanted my apology? He'd have to take it when I was darned good and ready to deliver said apology.

Inner bitch channeled, I charged down the hallway as though I had every right to be there. I tunneled my focus to the exit sign at the end of the narrow tube of a corridor. I managed to get about a quarter of the way to my destination before three shadow-looking figures sidestepped into my path. Guess they weren't shadows after all. Gulping, I rethought my strategy. They were massive and stunk like wet dog and stale cigarette smoke. Tribal tattoos—no carvings burned into their skin—ran along both sides of their faces, converging on their foreheads.

"I believe you're on the wrong floor, Riletta."

"H-how do you know my name?"

The man smirked and took a step toward me. "I know many things about you. I know you're going to be making me a very happy man tomorrow night."

Erm, no way in hell that's happening. I considered disagreeing, but silence seemed smarter, given the fact I was outnumbered three to one and by about seven hundred or so pounds.

"You don't look very convinced. Perhaps I should give you a sample?"

"No thanks. I'll just be surprised tomorrow." I forced my legs not to tremble and held my ground when he closed the scant distance between us. "Just out of curiosity, where exactly is said happiness going to take place? I don't want to be in the wrong place or anything."

He chuckled. The men behind him grinned, exposing rows of sharp, canine teeth. My stomach heaved. Hellhounds.

This wasn't good.

Jacob used to tell me stories about the hellhounds when I was really young. I still had nightmares.

"You are quite sweet, Riletta. Perhaps I will keep you after your champion is licking my feet to save your life."

"I'm afraid I'm not in the same conversation as you."

"Oh, but you are the conversation, my dear." He reached out to stroke my cheek, but I pulled back. "He didn't tell you, did he?"

I shook my head, not exactly sure who he was, even though my heart began a dull thud in my chest. Macen. "What did he do?"

"What he will do, my dear." He smirked as he adjusted his collar. "Tomorrow, your wolf champion will submit to my prowess in the ring before his entire pack and before all of Demonia. They will all see me turn him into my bitch."

The men beside him chuckled. A voice behind me boomed. "I do not recall approving this, Diego."

Diego's eyes narrowed. "Forgive me, Prince. The opportunity to weaken the Alpha's reputation came so quickly, I had to act. I'm sure you agree."

"Frankly, I agree with very little you do. Your pride swells your head so you only see past your nose. Many things are at play, and you are too ignorant to see that." Prince Drecor approached. He offered his hand. "Riletta, I assume."

"Yes, Prince. I was actually on my way to see you…to apologize for the inconvenience my stay has created." I swallowed and turned to face him fully, even though giving my back to Diego rankled something within me. "I wanted to offer my assurances I'll clear up the issues with ROAR and Macen as soon as I can. I know my assurances don't really mean much since you don't know me, but I've always believed a word is a bond, and it's not like I can do much else because Macen isn't even here, so I can't exactly get him to stop ROAR, and they won't talk to me about it because Macen's the one who started it and…."

I drew in a deep breath as I realized I'd lost my audience somewhere toward the start of the long, abrupt rambling. I had a tendency to do that when sheer terror grappled my mind. Everything came out as one giant glob with no filter, no order. No pause.

"I see. So, this arrangement I didn't agree to can't

happen because Macen isn't here because...."

"That's not relevant."

"I see." The prince released my hand—the one I hadn't realized he was touching. "You amuse me. No one ever says such things to me because everything is relevant if I ask. So, Diego, exactly why were you arranging this mock battle?"

"The wolf dared demand my assurance she would be safe within Ruger, like he commands the hellhounds."

The prince maneuvered me against the wall and stood nose-to-nose with Diego. This wasn't going to be good. I'd seen Jacob do this with the newer Alphas, the whelps who still needed to learn their place.

"And you think it's your place to decide this since you command the hellhounds?"

"Yes."

"I see." Flames shot forward before I could brace myself even though I expected a reaction. No leader worth his salt would take that sort of backtalk. Yes. Diego was an idiot.

I wanted to laugh. I wanted to scream and run. I wanted a lot of things but chose to remain still as stone and hope they forgot I was there. The flames incinerated Diego. He yelped and knelt, or tumbled, quickly. The fiery torment halted immediately.

Singed skin permeated the hallway with a disgusting stench I tried to ignore. The few seconds had destroyed his face, the skin sagged, black and peeling like an orange.

"Forgive me, Father."

Shit. Diego was his son? Jacob had nothing on the prince. Wow. I stepped back a bit as the fearful realization settled in me.

"I must deal with this mess you have created. Remain there and silent as I settle it. You have no idea what you've done." The prince turned and regarded me for a few moments.

The scrutiny made me shuffle from one foot to the other. I stared at the carpet; I studied the walls; I counted tiles. Finally, I looked at him. A malevolent grin spread across his face.

"My people are expecting a battle. My family will lose face if there isn't one, so you'll battle Diego's sisters. They're fierce warriors within their own right. You'll choose a champion to assist you in battle. A female champion."

Battle? Warriors?

Had I hit my head?

"Choose *now*."

Choose what? Oh, a champion. A female one. "I only know one female here. Well, I know two female wolves, but they don't like me much and—"

"Riletta, I tire of your drivel. Choose."

"I only know my roommate, Vira. I must talk to her first, though." Sure, I'd met a few other demons, but I barely knew their names. It wasn't like I could ask them to have my back.

"Vira will do quite nicely." He smirked. "We'll move the battle up to tonight, so no one decides to withdraw."

"I can't do this, Prince. I don't know how to battle. I'm not a warrior."

"I suggest you learn quickly." He looked around at everyone. "This will be much better. My daughters have the battle prowess my son lacks. He has yet to beat the wolf. It's a shame he'd resort to such tactics. I'm afraid my daughters will not need such antics, even with Vira in your corner."

Yeah, well, I was pretty sure they'd be mopping the floor with my blood easily enough. I had no options. All I could do was make sure this so-called battle helped Macen however it could. "If I do this, you'll forgive all issues you have with me and erase all debts and duties—perceived or otherwise—that Macen and his pack may have with you.

And you'll also owe them one debt, to be paid off at Macen's discretion. Agreed?"

The people around the prince gasped. Yeah, I was crazy for adding the last part, but it was worth a shot.

"This will help you save face with the wolf pack and your own people. That is worth one blood debt."

"You are a shrewd bargainer." The prince laughed. "Very well. I agree."

"Whether I win or lose."

"Whether you live or die."

Well, he didn't have to summarize it like that. Vira wasn't going to like this one bit. I guess she was right about staying on the first floor.

α

After Vira spent twenty minutes yelling at me and thirty minutes cursing at no one in particular, we had roughly three hours to turn my doughy softness into a hardened warrior able to kick the twin demon granddaughters of Satan himself.

Needless to say, I wasn't expecting much.

Vira was awesome—a female ninja, wolf warrior, and demon fighter all rolled into one. She taught through example because it was more effective. Personally, I was pretty sure she just wanted to kick my ass for getting her into this.

A couple of hours into it, I was deflecting most of her maneuvers and even scoring a few hits of my own. Every muscle in my body ached, and I was pretty sure I'd be bleeding from every orifice if she hadn't been holding back and not actually striking me.

She threw down the crazy double sword thingie she'd been wielding and glared at me. "If we survive this tonight, you and me are gonna talk about boundaries. You don't go dragging me into this shit. We clear?"

I nodded.

"Now that you have some basic moves, I'm hoping what I said earlier is beaten into your brain. What'd I say about the fight?"

"Don't get pissed. Getting pissed might make me shift, and if I'm what you think I am, that's not good." I swallowed and let loose my personal thoughts. "I don't think I'm that, you know. Whichever you're thinking. I'm nothing like that."

"That's not something we discuss here." She looked around the large, empty room. "After we get through this bullshit you got us into, we'll sit down with your man, my pop, and ROAR. We'll sort that shit out then, okay?"

I nodded.

"Now, remember never to turn your back on either of the twins. They are dirty fighters. We'll be tagging in and out, but the girl out on their side will be looking to strike if we let our guard down. We won't be doing that, right?"

I shook my head. No guard down. Done.

"That what you're fighting in?"

I looked down at my white tee and gray yoga pants. They both hung loosely on me. "It's what I have."

She sighed and looked up to the sky as though speaking to some higher power, which was nuts since she was from down there. I wanted to point that out, but, again, silence was worth more than words at this point.

"I really appreciate this," I whispered. "I'm sorry you got dragged in. Really. I couldn't think about Macen dealing with this when he got back from dealing with his parents' deaths."

"You didn't share that tidbit with them, did you?"

"No." My eyes widened. "I shouldn't have told you."

"I won't say shit. Macen and his crew saved my dumb ass awhile back. You're the debt I'm paying, but I think tonight gets me an extra favor. Or two." She picked up a triple knifed thingie with a curved, wooden handle. "You have any experience in battle?"

"No. I used to watch the training field of my pack from behind a bush. I spent hours watching, trying to absorb the knowledge."

"Why?"

"I'd be alone eventually. I needed to know how to defend myself. I didn't want to die." The last sentence came out as a soft whisper, a barely audible exposure of my deepest secret.

I was terrified.

"You have good instincts and excellent reaction times. Trust your gut and your impulses. Shut down your mind, and you'll be fine." She tossed a pair of leather pants and a black top at me. "Change into this. It's showtime."

I changed quickly, ignoring the pangs of unease weighing down my limbs. The dull throb of overused muscles settled my mind somehow. They proved I could handle it.

Maybe.

I followed Vira and dutifully got on the back of her Harley, grabbing the bar behind me. The ride to Temple took less time than I'd hoped. She wove around the massive swell of parked vehicles and parked beside the side exit.

I jumped off and removed my helmet.

"If things go south, we're heading here and booking it. We need to get notice to whoever from Macen's pack is here tonight that we may need their help getting out if shit goes down." She settled her helmet on the handlebar and handed me a knife. "Put this in your boot, just in case. It's coated with phoenix blood and is fatal to demons."

"Phoenix blood?" That was one of the species she'd mentioned earlier. "What are they? I tried to find stuff about them at the library, but there was nothing."

"Info about them is restricted because it tends to freak my kind out. It's an ancient shifter race that straddled the line between the Earthen realm and Demonia. They ensured our races got along. They could kill anyone and anything."

"What happened to them?"

"Some say a higher power believed they wielded too much power and slaughtered them all."

"That's horrible."

"Yeah. And to think humans think angels are good."

"Wait. Angels slaughtered the phoenixes?"

"Yep. That's one of the beliefs."

"What's the other?"

"That they were equals, both straddling the realms. They grew bored with the foolishness of our worlds and vanished, choosing to deal with more worthy issues."

"I like that belief better."

"I figured you would." She looked around. "If we're done with ancient history, I think we've got some demon twins to school."

The crowd was thick, a crushing mass of doom. No matter what happened, tonight would end badly. There were too many wolves here, too many demons, and no order within the chaos.

A barbed-wire cage was in the center of the room. "What is that?"

"Our fighting arena."

"Wait. We're going to be inside a cage?"

"Yeah."

I shook my head.

"I didn't mention that." It was a statement in an "oops" sort of tone.

I didn't do cages. Ever. Not since.... "I can't do a cage. I have issues with confined spaces."

"And I have issues with dying." Vira poked my chest and growled. "Get over it."

Oookay. Sure.

"You show your thoughts on your face. You want to

live through tonight, stop doing it."

Alrighty. Easy. Peasy.

She grabbed my arm and dragged me toward the cage. I ignored the barbs and verbal jibes tossed our direction from the demons. Most of them were directed at Vira. Apparently, siding with me wasn't earning her any popularity points.

"Sorry. I didn't realize they'd hate you for doing this for me."

"No skin off me. They hated me to start with. Deciding to live on Earth wasn't exactly the popular choice."

"How did that happen?"

"My dad was an ambassador."

"That must've sucked."

"Yeah." She shrugged. "You can't let the past rule you."

True enough. I took a deep breath and stared at the cage. I could do this. I had to. This would help Macen and his pack. Assuming I survived, my slate would be clear with Demonia and, hopefully, the dean. All would be well. I could move on with my new freedom.

"Riles, what the hell do you think you're doing?" Lane grabbed my other arm. His hot breath fanned my forehead. "You're coming with me."

"Afraid not, big boy."

He vanished before me. I blinked and looked at the mass of man at my feet.

Vira straddled his prone form. "Don't touch her."

"Ease off, Vira. He's with me." Logan crossed his arms and glared at me. "And he had an excellent question. What the hell are you doing, Riles?"

"What I have to. This clears the slate."

"You believe that shit?"

"He gave his word." I think. I couldn't remember the exact words. "Macen had no right to enter a fight agreement on my behalf to begin with. I am not pack. I'm not his to protect."

"Oh, really?" Lane grunted from under Vira's foot. "You don't let me up, little demon, and I'm spanking your ass all night then spreading your legs and fucking you raw."

Vira purred. "Don't promise what you can't deliver, big boy. I like it rougher than you do."

He growled, and Vira yelped as he dragged her down and flipped her beneath him with a speed which defied my gaze. I blinked. Wow.

"Don't promise what you can't deliver, little demon."

"Why don't we save your energy for the ring?"

The new voice startled me. I drew closer to Logan as I regarded Prince Drecor, who smirked at Lane and Vira when they leaped to their feet quickly.

Vira bowed even though she glared. "My Prince."

"You honor me with your willingness to champion Riletta."

"I do it for her, not you. And the name is Riles, not Riletta."

"Whatever the reason, I am grateful nonetheless. I have spoken with my daughters and requested they not draw too much blood." He shrugged. "I'm afraid that only heightened their bloodlust. They rarely do as I request. My apologies in advance."

"And I shall extend mine in advance because I'm honor bound to defend my charge to the death," Vira stated. "Regardless of the threat."

"I would expect no less from Rolanzo's bloodline. Watching you in the ring will be an experience for us all." He smiled when he regarded Logan and Lane. "I'm saddened Macen was unable to attend. Riletta is quite the negotiator, though. After tonight, all debts owed by your pack are erased, and a blood debt is now owed to you."

Both the men glared at me, their jaws twitching. "Why

would you agree to that, Prince?"

"She was the only one brave enough to dare such a request. Her innocence amused me."

"Macen will draw blood when he learns of this fight," Logan said. "Females don't fight."

"They do tonight." The prince looked over his shoulder. "It appears my daughters are ready."

I looked behind me. Holy shit. Two women with long, black hair in braids shoved their way through the crowd. Towering over the audience, they were easily over six and a half feet. At five foot one inch, I was intimidated by their muscular bodies. Their legs were thick like redwoods in California. Their shoulders rivaled linebackers.

What the hell had I gotten us into?

The situation went from bad to worse because Vira was too good. That didn't make sense, but it was true. Apparently, knocking out one of the twin hellhounds within a minute of the battle's start was a bad idea.

Things got real bad after that. Vira had set an ugly, in-your-face tone I lacked the proficiency to deliver. I watched her crush both twins as they changed fighters often. Guilt made me wish I had more to offer, that I could relieve her. I wasn't stupid. Even exhausted, she was better than I would be.

Vira kicked one of them into the cage's side, knocking her out, but she tapped her twin in. The other sister slammed Vira against the barbed wire cage and sneered when she slid to the floor, blood oozing down her face. A burst of fiery hellfire engulfed the corner.

I bit my tongue, swallowing the scream in my throat. Vira's words of wisdom ran on a steady, calming loop in my mind.

They'll fight with hellfire. I can survive it; you might not. If you're what we're thinking you are, you'd survive, but they'd kill you anyway. Either way, you die.

She would be okay. She had to be.

I gulped and entered the fray. I couldn't hang back and watch Vira be destroyed because of me. Logan and Lane prowled within my field of vision with a massive pack of wolves behind them. I could do this.

For Macen.

I hadn't bothered learning my competitors' names. I didn't care. They were a problem—one I had to handle. My current opponent circled me with a sneer on her face and amusement in her eyes. Once again, I was a joke. Anger rose within me, a slow burn radiating from my belly and fanning out within my blood.

"You're going to bleed and hurt so bad you won't even yelp like the bitch you are." The hellhound took a few steps forward and brandished a double-tipped sword. Good. I'd practiced fending that thingie off. I could do this.

Anger keeps them off center. Piss them off however you can. I looked over to the empty corner. Good. She'd moved.

"I'm not a wolf, you dumb cow."

She lunged. I ducked to the side and jumped into the defensive stance Vira had taught me. I kept my weight on the balls of my feet, my limbs loose and ready for the next attack.

She shot a stream of hellfire toward me. I leaped backward and winced when the edge of her weapon sliced a long, thin path along my forearm. That'd teach me to move faster. I blocked the next attack with my injured arm, shoving her backward.

An ear-piercing howl thickened the tension. The crowd growled and screamed. The woman fell to her knees and yelled louder, calling out to her father, begging for mercy. What the hell?

Shit.

Whatever you do, don't let your blood touch them.

Something within me stirred, a persistent rustling

along my skin. The second twin appeared in the arena. Her eyes widened when she knelt beside her sister. Rage mottled her features when she stood and faced me. Both her arms rose.

I anticipated hellfire, but I was wedged in a corner. I couldn't run. My skin burned, prickled with tiny shards of pain along my spine. My vision narrowed, contorted to an iridescent tunnel focused on the fiery flames surging toward me.

Growls erupted around me. Pain coursed along my skin, tiny pinpricks followed by crunching pain along my joints. This was it. My death. I'd failed.

I'm sorry, Macen.

Chapter Nine

Macen

I'd made a five-hour drive in two and burned out a Harley along the way. Pissed, exhausted, and on edge, I shoved my way into Temple. What the fuck was Riles thinking? Why the hell had Prince Drecor agreed to this bullshit?

Why had my pack done nothing?

My wolf growled and snarled at anyone who looked my direction. The clustered crowd parted when I made my way toward the cage. Fuck. I was too late to stop the craziness.

Riles was soft, sweet innocence. She had no business in any battle, much less this one. A pained howl from within the battle zone rose above the agitated observers. Riles stood in a corner, watching the two twins with wide, confused eyes. I sensed the terror burgeoning within the demon masses but couldn't figure out why.

I stopped beside Logan. "What the hell is going on?"

"No clue. Riles blocked a move, and the hellhound just went down, yowling like she'd been ripped open."

"Fuck," Lane growled as he lunged toward the cage. "Hellfire."

I lunged for the barbed wire, tugging and pulling at the locked entry as the other twin stood and focused her rage on Riles.

"Run, Riles. Get the fuck out of there." There was nowhere to go. I struggled with the lock, trying to rip it open. Blood ran along my arms. "Get this lock off. Now."

Flames erupted within the cage. My heart seized. My wolf raged.

Fuck, no. This wasn't happening.

I'm sorry, Macen.

Riles. The soft whisper within my mind, filled with anguish and regret, made my wolf howl in desperation as I fell to my knees, forced to helplessly watch the hellfire like a neutered mutt.

They would all die for this. Every last fucking demon would die.

Shards of iridescent light fractured the flames until beams of blinding white exploded outward, engulfing the hellfire and the twins. Demons screamed. My pack growled their confusion and shifted. Logan appeared in my peripheral vision. Covered in blood, he undid the lock to the cage. I lunged into the arena, unable to see past the blinding, swirling, white and blue shroud of light.

It enveloped the area, a thick blanket of power so strong I dropped my head, too weakened to move. Logan and Lane stumbled beside me.

What the fuck?

Vira crawled to us, pain etched on her bloodied face. Lane tugged her to us.

"Get her out of here before the prince summons his army." She clawed at my arm. "Hide her."

"What the hell is going on?"

"Later. Not here." She swallowed. "Go. She must be protected. They'll destroy her."

The urgency in her voice strengthened me. Was Riles alive? The light dulled, and the power dissipated enough to expose a pair of white angelic wings with rays of blue and gold wrapped around a blue and gold bird. A patch of white ran along her neck.

She was beautiful.

Riles. My heart beat wildly as I waited for proof that what I'd sensed before was true. *Heart mate. Speak to me. Please.*

Macen?

I'm here, mouse. Come back to me.

W-what happened? What am I?

We'll figure it out together. Come back to me, Riles. Vira's urgency returned to the forefront of my mind when my pack growled from the exterior of the cage. Their surrounding presence would only hold back the demons for so long.

How?

Imagine yourself calm, safe in my arms. Your animal will release its hold when you are calm.

I'm never calm in your arms. You ignite me.

The confession undid me. I got closer until I could brush my hands along her soft down. *You're gorgeous, Riles.*

The light swelled once more. Temporarily blinded, I looked away until it disappeared entirely.

Riles lay crumped beside me, curled into a fetal position which covered her nakedness. Her ebony hair pooled around her shoulders. I removed my jacket and slowly helped her until I could zip the leather covering closed. Lifting her up, I headed for the exit.

Secure our exit.

Most of the amassing demons leaped backward when we approached, their eyes widened. Whatever the hell this was, they knew more than I did, and that didn't make my wolf happy.

I set Riles down on wobbly legs, not trusting myself to speak right now. Fuck, she was all soft and innocent sweetness wrapped in my jacket. It enveloped her fully, barely covering her delectable ass and sweet pussy. I didn't want the bastards here seeing her like this—utterly fuckable. *Mine.* My wolf prowled too close to the surface, demanding control over the situation. I needed to secure her. Now.

Straddling Lane's bike, I looked at her. "Get on."

Her warmth against my back calmed me enough to get us away from the threat. I took to the highway with no destination. Concerned about Riles, I stopped at a motel about an hour away. It'd have to do.

A couple of hundred bucks ensured our privacy in the back of the unit. The moment the door shut, I pulled her into my arms. Her weight settled against me. The heat from her body made my dick harden.

"Macen, please." She pulled at my shirt, dragging my face down until her lips feathered against mine. "Please. I need you."

I understood the need. The adrenaline rush of battle mixed with the primal melding with your inner beast did things to a person, made them wanton. The kiss was possessive, the claiming I'd wanted for days. She tasted like ambrosia, a drug I wanted more than air as my tongue dueled with hers.

Tentative hands swept beneath my shirt, squeezing and flexing until I groaned and shed the unwanted layer between us. I fumbled with the jacket's zipper, gently caressing her pale, ivory skin as it fell into view.

My mouth dried, and my body heated when Riles ran her hands along my arms and chest. A sexy, pinky tinge colored her cheeks.

Looking up at me through half-hooded eyes, she whispered, "I could touch you all night and never grow bored."

"We have a lifetime." The truth settled in my soul. She was mine. I was hers.

Heart mates.

My heart thumped wildly beneath her hand. "Make me yours, Macen, even if it's only for tonight."

An eternity wouldn't be enough. I growled against her neck, inhaling the sweet ambrosia. She tasted like tangy vanilla with a splash of cinnamon. I settled her into my embrace and claimed her lips, sweeping my tongue into her mouth. I kissed each bruise softly, somewhat surprised at how remarkably fast she'd healed since we'd left the battle.

Her animal was strong, whatever it was.

I carried her to the bed and settled my weight above her. I wanted to plunge into her, feel her moist heat wrapped tightly around my aching dick. Later.

The son of a bitch in me would have to deal with blue balls a little longer because I wouldn't rush this. My vision blurred as my wolf prowled closer.

"I-I shouldn't do this, not when I don't even know what I am. What's going to happen to me?" The fear-filled whisper made me growl. "I need to talk to Vira. I should've listened to her. She was right. I'm something from there, that place she told me about. I need Vira."

"Vira is in recovery. We can't talk to her. I don't like you afraid." I feathered kisses along her face. None of what she was saying made much sense, but I didn't give a rat's ass what she was or wasn't. All that mattered was she was mine, and she was safe. "Forget about everything but us, Riles. We'll figure everything out tomorrow."

I lost myself in her velvety kiss, the friction of skin against skin as I tasted her neck, her breasts. Her nipples pebbled beneath my fingers. Soft gasps of pleasure mingled with my needy groans.

I growled when she turned us over so she was straddling me. I could smell her arousal in my nostrils along with her moist need when she writhed against the prominent bulge in my jeans.

Riles leaned down. Her soft lips ran along my skin as though she would taste every inch of me. I could count on one hand how many times a woman had done this—spent time on the niceties of foreplay. Female wolves weren't into this sort of thing.

Arousal burst in me, tiny explosive landmines beneath my skin wherever she touched, kissed. She paused, licking and kneading my arms. "I can sense your wolf. He's close."

"He wants you."

"Good. I want him," she whispered. She undid my belt and jeans. Doubt broke through the haze of desire in her gaze. "I'm not.... This isn't something I do a lot. Well, never. I mean, I'm not a.... You're the first I wanted."

Rage rose within me, but I fought to remain calm. I'd kill all those who'd hurt her later. Tonight, I'd kiss the hurt in her eyes away and make love to her until the doubt in her voice gave way to cries of pleasure.

Sensing her need to control the pace, I lifted my hips and allowed her to remove the rest of my clothes. Desire was evident in the golden flecks of her gaze. She licked her lips as she wrapped her hand around my dick. I grunted, encouraging her tentative strokes by thrusting my hips to set a rhythm she learned quickly.

I ran my hands down her sides, pausing to pay homage to her gorgeous tits. She thrust herself into my palms. I flicked her sensitive nipples until she bit down on her lower lip and rubbed her wet pussy against my aching dick.

Fuck.

"Touch yourself for me, mouse."

Lust seized me. A slight tremble in her hands made protectiveness swell in me. She took my hands and ran them along her body, pausing on her breasts.

"I like when you squeeze me here."

"Oh, yeah?"

"Yes."

I complied until she gasped and settled on me until her wet heat was snuggled against my raging dick.

Jesus, this was killing me.

"Show me where you want me to taste you, sweetness."

She sighed and ran her hands along her ribs, down her hips. One hand wrapped around my dick, and the other moved to the slickened folds of her pussy. I couldn't breathe, too enraptured by the lust pounding in my blood, the need to taste her there, feel her release.

Her arousal glimmered on her fingertips when she drew them away. Pupils dilated, she brushed them across my lips. I suckled them hungrily, lapping at the evidence of her need. The hand around my dick squeezed as she rose above me.

I growled and flipped us. "I need you now, Riles. Let me have all of you."

"Macen." Her legs settled around me, her fingers dug into my shoulders as she claimed my mouth in a hungry kiss. "Make me yours. Please."

I melted into the kiss and slid into her. Swallowing her gasp, I groaned at the heat, the firm grip of her pussy around my dick. I remained fully seated, unmoving, even though I wanted to thrust, fuck her long, hard, and deep until we both collapsed in exhaustion.

Her fingernails dug into my shoulders, her skin heated beneath me. My wolf groaned when her animal prowled to the surface. "Fuck me, Macen."

I fucked her hard and fast. Sweat coated my skin.

She licked my neck and moaned. "Salty."

Jesus.

She met me, thrust for thrust, our breathing labored and our bodies gliding against one another. I nipped at her neck until she stilled beneath me.

"Mine." The growl rumbled in my throat long after the

word hung between us.

"Yes," she whispered. "Always yours."

I wanted to turn her over, take possession the way my wolf demanded. Next time. Riles tensed beneath me. She clawed and scraped her nails along my skin, clinging to me as she spiraled into her release.

I slowed my thrusts, rubbing her clit with my finger as I looked down at her. "Look at me, Riles."

Her eyes fluttered open, and I was lost in the passionate sea of endless golden-flecked blue. My balls tightened; my body tensed. I needed her release more than I needed the ragged breaths I dragged into my lungs.

"Come with me, Riles."

She clung to me. Body tensed, I inhaled her succulent scent and lost myself in her release. Fire spread through me. My wolf fractured, undone by the emotions enveloping us. A woman had never meant this much to me, never been everything I wanted. Needed.

I claimed her mouth, growling my release as we both collapsed in a sweaty tangle of limbs. As I battled to find some semblance of breath, I silently prayed to whatever god heard me that I hadn't lied to her. Things had to be right tomorrow. I couldn't lose her. Not now. Not ever.

I drew her into my arms and kissed her forehead. She sighed and lazed by my side like a contented kitten. I had a thousand questions, but exhaustion and euphoria took over. For the first time in years, my wolf settled, calmed by the fact we'd found his mate.

My mate.

My Riles.

ᣳ

Riles

Something within me shifted, prowling to the surface

once again. The sensation was unsettling, yet calming. I'd shifted.

I'd killed.

Shock kept me silent and still within Macen's embrace. His heat blanketed me. The steady breathing eased the apprehensive pangs crawling through my mind. Shards of last night pieced themselves together, offering a larger picture I didn't want to deal with.

I'd inhaled hellfire.

How was that even possible? What had I shifted into? I remember the crunch of bone, the flickering flames within my blood. Obviously, Vira had been right. I was an angel. Or a phoenix. Or something from that world. I needed answers that I suspected wouldn't make anything to come simpler. People feared different—I'd dealt with it all my life without understanding how truly weird I was compared to everyone else.

I was an abomination just like Jacob always said.

All I could do now was get answers and hope Macen would understand. I couldn't imagine losing him. Carefully extricating myself from his arms, I padded into the motel's dingy bathroom and stared into the mirror.

The bruises I'd expected were almost healed. At least I'd gotten the benefits of being a shifter. What would happen to me now? I'd killed those twins. Their screams echoed in my mind.

I'd have to turn myself in. But to who? Although it killed me to imagine, I had to distance myself from Macen. I couldn't allow him or his pack—either of his packs—to be damaged by what I'd done last night.

Warm hands drifted along my thighs and wrapped around my waist. I closed my eyes and leaned into Macen's strength. For this moment, I'd pretend it was all okay, that he was truly mine, and we'd have an eternity together. My nostrils and eyes burned; my vision clouded when I blinked.

"I can't help you if you don't let me in, Riles. We're in this together, mouse. From here on out. We clear?"

I nodded and squeezed his hand. "I'm scared, Macen. What will happen to me? Oh, God! I killed someone last night. Two someones."

The pain spewed from me, and I collapsed, my knees too weak to support the weight of what I'd done. I couldn't make something so malevolent right. "I didn't know. I didn't know I had that in me. God, I should've stopped it somehow. They died because of me."

"I've got you, sweetheart." Macen picked me up and carried to the bed.

Even though I sat in his lap like a petulant child, I leaned into him, somewhat calmed by the soothing glide of his hand down my arm and the rich timbre of his voice. I couldn't process the words. They were nonsense which couldn't withstand the pounding terror and pain within my mind.

I sat there, rocking gently in his embrace until reality intruded. A firm knock on the door startled me to standing.

"Hey." Macen palmed my chin and lifted until I locked gazes with him. "It's going to be okay. You're mine. I won't let anyone hurt you ever again."

Nodding, I silently hoped he was right. I'd never had anyone in my corner before.

I had to admit it felt damn good. I slid on his shirt from the night before, pausing briefly to inhale his scent, a succulent ambrosia that awakened the need within me.

He opened the door and growled as he stepped back. "This couldn't wait until after we had breakfast?"

"Funny. I thought that's what we were bringing." Logan entered, carrying fast food bags. The aroma made my stomach rumble. Lane followed with a holder loaded down with steaming coffee. "Hey, Riles."

Okay. I'd morphed into a hideous creature straight from a horror novel, barbequed two demons, and all I got was a "Hey, Riles"? I'd expected accusations, anger. I'd dragged the pack into a heap of mess last night with what I'd done.

"She okay?" Lane pulled the table from the wall until the left side of the bed could serve as seating. He positioned the two chairs around the other side of the small circular surface. It was downright homey.

"She's fine," I responded. "I just have a lot on my mind. I'm sorry about last night. I'm not sure what the hell happened."

"Well, we may have a few answers for you." Logan sat and reached into the massive bag. "Sit, eat. We got you a veggie omelet with hash browns and pancakes. Lane thought you'd want toast, but that's for pansies. Pancakes with syrup rock, right?" He winked and pushed the food toward the other end of the table.

I sat beside Macen, who smirked at his second.

"Thanks for the food, man."

He shrugged. "Gotta eat. No biggie."

I ate with abandon as though it was my last meal. For all I knew it was. I shoveled, not giving a damn what the two men across from me thought. Macen understood. We'd burned a lot of calories through the night.

Heat rose in my cheeks when I looked over at him. I'd awakened him several times, too wanton for his touch to sleep. The animal within me stirred and hummed in awareness. I could sense Macen's wolf.

My mate.

"You learn anything after we took off last night?"

"Yeah, hellhounds don't take too kindly to the shit that went down last night." Lane mouthed a bite of egg and chewed for a bit. "Your girl here scared the piss out of them."

"I did?" I choked a bit on my hash browns. "Why?"

"Also learned Vira can kick Stacy's ass without even blinking. You should've seen her. Man, it was beautiful.

Even half dead, that vampire demon was fierce." Logan laughed. "Sorry, we're getting ahead of ourselves. We figured Vira knew more than we did, and we were right. Come to find out, your girl is either a phoenix or an angel. Or both. Vira thinks both."

"What the hell?" Macen shoved his food aside and leaned forward. "Explain."

"Apparently, it was pretty common knowledge a century or so ago that angels and phoenixes straddled the lines between Earth and Demonia, proverbial guardians to ensure neither side had too much power. They kept shit from hitting the fan, so to speak," Lane said.

"Then they gave up, went away, or just didn't give a shit anymore. No one really knows." Logan shrugged. "All the demons knew is they weren't there anymore. They were forgotten in our realm but became the stuff of childhood stories to keep the little demons in line."

"Why were they afraid of them?"

"They could strike down a full-fledged demon with a drop of phoenix blood or a burst of angel fire."

"And that's what I am."

"Based on what we figured out, yes." Kindness reflected in Lane's gaze. "You've created quite a stir. No one knows exactly what to think about you. Fortunately, we contacted some elders. A couple of them seemed to know more about these two species. They apparently had strict upbringings and adhered to a regimented tradition— one that dwindled their races to almost nonexistence.

"Just over a century ago, new leadership took control of their realm. The decision was made to sever all ties with and responsibilities to Earth and Demonia, to focus on their world and problems rather than handling ours."

"So, how did I land here?"

Lane sighed and looked at Logan with darkness on his face. "We've gotta tell her, man."

"It took some digging, a lot of phone calls, and a shit

load of favors being called in by every pack we had alliances with. We finally got a way to connect with the new leader. He listened to what we had to say, and then he abruptly announced he'd call us back." Lane sighed. "We heard from him an hour ago. It's been a long night."

"A fucking long ass night. We've had the entire pack and every pack we were from up making calls country wide." Logan leaned back into his chair. "Thank fuck it paid off."

"What did he say?"

"He found your parents."

Chapter Ten

It'd been a hectic, yet glorious, week. Macen insisted I move into Wolf Hall. Although most of the pack embraced my presence, there was a thick tension between Stacy and myself as well as the few of her crew who hadn't abandoned her. Rules were fuzzy about mated Alphas in residence at the dorm and whether that made their mate the head female.

I'd assured Macen and Stacy and everyone who'd listen I didn't want to be Alpha female. I wasn't pack. I was Macen's mate, and I wanted nothing to detract from my new role. His family pack embraced me fully—I had so many family members now I couldn't keep count, much less remember their names.

Vira had become my shadow. The guilt had slowly started giving way to the acceptance that I couldn't change how horridly I'd screwed up her life. All of Demonia hated her—she'd been found guilty of the death of Prince Drecor's daughters and banished to the Earthen realm permanently.

"Stop thinking about that shit." She slapped my hand. "And stop fiddling with your top. You look gorgeous, and fuck them if what you wear matters. They're lucky this shit is even going down."

"Vira, we discussed this. What happened in Jacob's pack wasn't their fault. They weren't there."

"Exactly. They. Weren't. There." Her obsidian eyes sparkled with red. "They should've been, and until I hear for myself why the fuck they weren't, every second of what went down with that miserable prick's pack is their fault as far as I'm concerned."

To say she'd become rather protective of me was an understatement. Macen found it amusing. I found it a bit overwhelming. She was my sister in every way that mattered. I wanted to thank her, tell her I loved her and felt the same protectiveness she did. I was pretty sure she wasn't prepared for my emotional diarrhea.

"I still say we should've made them wait longer."

"It's been a week." I took a deep breath. "Honestly, I can't wait any longer. I want answers, Vira."

"We all do." She squeezed my shoulder. "Let's go. They're waiting."

They. My parents. My animal stirred in my belly. I followed her down the stairs to the bottom level of Wolf Hall. Sharing a room with Macen had made me nervous at first, but I'd wanted to be with him, in his bed.

His mate.

"I hope Macen gets back in time to be here with us."

"He just arrived." Vira grinned when I looked over my shoulder. "I've got really good hearing."

I was a bit jealous since I had something in me. I didn't know how to communicate with the thing inside me. I didn't understand what it could do, what it wanted from our relationship. It sounded foolish, but it was how I'd heard many shifters describe their inner animal. Hopefully, today would give me some answers, some idea how to delve into my powers.

If I had any.

We entered Macen's office. A trio stood—a petite woman with long, flaxen hair and shimmering sky blue eyes. Her soft smile trembled as she gripped the man beside her. He wrapped his arms around her, and his cautious, green eyes tracked my movement into the room. His ebony hair matched mine. He was tall with wide shoulders and a massive torso to rival Macen's.

A younger, slender, flaxen-haired woman stood beside them. This was my sister. Macen made his way to me, encircling me in his strength. The thing inside me stirred, humming softly in pleasure. My heart fluttered.

"Xenia," the woman whispered.

"Betina, we discussed this," the man whispered. "She is Riletta."

"Riles," Macen corrected.

"Of course, forgive me." The woman approached, her arm extended. "You are more beautiful than I could've imagined."

"Don't hover. You're making her nervous." The man smiled. "I am Savan, and this is my mate, Betina. This is our other daughter, Xandra."

Xandra stepped forward. "So, you're my little sister. We thought you were dead."

Betina gasped.

"Xandra, we discussed this. We curb frankness in this realm. It's often not appreciated." Savan grinned. "My apologies."

They'd discussed this. They'd discussed *me*. Then they cared, right? "It's nice to meet you."

"Sit, please." Lane motioned toward the sofa.

Macen and I took the chair beside them. He settled me next to him and wrapped his arms around me.

Lane leaned against the desk. "Vira and I are here as intermediaries, if you will."

The smirk on his face made me grin. They were far from neutral.

"Thank you for all you did for X— Riletta. *Riles*." Savan sighed. "This is still quite a shock to us. When my uncle contacted me, I couldn't believe you were alive."

"Your uncle?"

"Yes, the king. He was the one Lane spoke with. We have claims almost daily since we've never stopped searching for you," Betina explained.

"You were stolen from our bedchamber by a disgruntled heir of the former king. We tracked him down a couple of months after your disappearance, but he never gave us your location. He died during questioning a year after we captured him." Savan squeezed Betina's hand when she leaned against him. "We've heard very little about your upbringing."

"I was found in the woods. Jacob's pack took me in." What more was there to say?

Tears glimmered in their gazes.

"They should know it all, Riles. They'll want to know," he whispered.

I couldn't. Not now. Probably not ever. Their suffering was too deep, too real for me to compound it with a past I'd already written off. None of it mattered since I was with Macen now.

"You are mated to an Alpha wolf," Xandra commented. "Uncle Lucian won't appreciate that."

"Who she mates is hardly *Uncle Lucian's* business," Macen growled. "Continue with that judgmental tone, and this is over before it starts. She's been through hell because of all this. I won't have my heart mate hurting."

"Amen," Vira said. "I'll show them out."

"You befriended a demon vampiress. Interesting." Xandra prowled toward my friend. "How did that happen?"

"That's not your business," Vira said.

"I'm a shifter?" The obvious shift in conversation worked.

Xandra returned to her spot on the sofa, and Vira was shoved back to her position against the desk by a glaring

Lane. Macen chuckled and kissed my shoulder.

"Based on what we've been told, you are like Xandra, a blend of phoenix and angel. It is a rare and quite powerful beast. Once we have you back at home, we will be able to train you on how to communicate and work with your animal properly." Savan smiled. "You are from two of the strongest bloodlines of our kind. Our mating was a shock within our land. Angels didn't mate with phoenixes."

Macen tensed beneath me. "Rewind that a bit. Once you have her back at home?"

"Of course. We can't condone her existence here until she's been properly trained and educated. It is for your safety as much as hers," Betina said.

"Not happening," Macen growled.

"It isn't up for discussion," Savan replied.

"I agree. It isn't." Lane crossed his arms. "You are here by invitation. She is the heart mate to an Alpha within one of the largest, fiercest packs around. She isn't going anywhere."

"Men," Xandra sighed. "If it is okay with you, Macen, I will remain here and train your Riles myself. It will give us time to bond."

"You have a wedding to plan," Betina said.

"I had no say in the groom. Why should I have any say in your grand merger?" Xandra retorted.

"You seek sanctuary with my pack?"

"Yes, in exchange for my training your mate. My sister." Xandra ignored the startled gasps of her parents. "Please."

"Xandra. This is hardly the place to air your concerns with your destiny." Betina reached for her daughter.

"My *destiny* is a sixty year old, pockmarked, freak of nature who thinks I look good in bondage chains. I think this is the perfect time to air my concerns since I'll hardly get the chance when we leave." Xandra crossed her arms.

"So? Do you agree?"

"It's your call, Riles." Macen's voice was a husky whisper against my neck.

My parents were forcing my sister to marry an old man? How was that possible? I didn't know any of them. How could I take a side?

I sighed and stood, placing myself between my newfound sister and the two people who birthed me. "I refuse to take a side and get dragged into whatever is going on between you. Xandra, I would love for you to be a guest of my mate's pack, but I will not have him protecting you from whatever you are running from.

"Betina and Savan, I would love the opportunity to get to know you two, but I will not risk my new pack. It sounds as though there are many things at play I am not aware of. This might sound harsh, but I don't care. Macen is my family. I will have my own children—hopefully, soon. My heart is filled with love for the people in this room. I want you to be part of that, but not at their expense."

Betina's eyes filled with tears. Savan nodded as he stood. "You are as fierce as your mother."

"I'm looking forward to seeing that for myself."

"As am I." Savan looked over at Xandra. "Daughter of mine, you have never once revealed your thoughts about this impending marriage to me. It is my fault for not asking. Forgive me. I will speak with your uncle and address the issue. I believe your training your sister and remaining here in the Earthen realm is a perfect temporary solution. I am proud of you for taking a stand even though it was far from the appropriate time."

"Thank you, Father."

"Never thank me for being your father." He looked at me. "We look forward to getting to know you, Riles. Your animal has chosen its mate wisely. Macen is a fierce protector. It will be an honor for our family to be aligned with such a strong pack."

Although I wanted my newfound family to stay, this was a process. I wanted to know more, learn about my animal and the world I'd been ripped from. I wasn't ready. I wanted to cement my place within Macen's pack, my new family, first.

My mind shut down as we bid them goodbye. Xandra would be returning soon to train me. I looked forward to it even if I had no clue what to expect. I figured it couldn't be much worse than what Vira had been putting me through.

Macen dragged me up the stairs. I laughed softly when he tugged me into our room and slammed the door. The lock fell into place. I sighed, inhaling the musky scent of my mate. I recognized the arousal now, the flare of need which hung between us.

He flipped me around until my face was pressed against the wall. I groaned at the brush of cool air when my skirt was hiked up. "Gotta say, mouse. Your sweet little talk about kids, our *family,* made me hornier than hell."

"Macen."

Deft fingers plunged into my pussy. "I love how wet you get for me." He nipped my neck. "I love you, mouse."

"Riles. The mouse is retiring."

"Mmm. Gotta say, sweetheart, I'm loving your animal. I can't wait to see you training, learning to defend our family. But I'll always have your back. You're mine." He thrust into me.

I gasped as pleasure swirled within me. His hands grasped my hips, held me in place as he pounded into me. His arousal excited me, made my pulse race and my body tremble.

His hands commanded my body, grazing my clit and then maneuvering under my top to tease my hard nipples. He pinched until I emitted the soft groan which made his wolf growl in response.

God, I loved this man.

"Macen, please."

"Please what?"

"I need to come. Please."

"I've got you, Riles." He thrust deep into me and flicked my clit once more. I fell apart in his arms, drifting in the riptide of sensations rushing through me. He growled in my ear and relaxed against me, his labored breaths mingling with mine. "Fuck, that was hot, sweetheart."

I sighed. "Yeah, it was."

He kissed me tenderly when I turned around. His mouth was a registered weapon as far as I was concerned. I focused on my mate.

"Can't do this much longer, Riles. They're expecting us up north."

Oh, yeah. Up north. "Mmm. Does that mean I can play with you on the way?"

"Those hands of yours kill me when you're on the back of my bike, babe." He nibbled my ear. "We have an eternity to play."

Yes. We did.

"Are you going to tell them about your plan?" I drew away and studied his face. "I know you're worried how they'll react."

"They'll accept it. I'm their Alpha now, but I'm not ready for that pack. It's too big, and it's in the middle of a lot of shit because of my father's rein. Gramps is a damn good Alpha. He stepped down before he should've. He'll do right by them."

"You'll be ready soon. I have to admit I love the fact you'll be here at the university, but I was serious. I'll be just as happy up there as I am here. I go where you go. You are my life. My family."

"And you're mine. I won't have you sacrificing what

you want. I know how much these classes mean to you."

"I forget how well you know me."

He grinned. "Then I guess I need to remind you tonight. Repeatedly."

"Promises. Promises." I squealed when he tickled my sides. "Okay, okay. I'm at your mercy."

"Mmm, you will be tonight." He kissed my throat. Tingles shot through my core. "And every night. You'll never be alone again, Riles."

I didn't know what to do with that. The impact of his words, the security they offered, terrified me almost as much as they thrilled me. Losing him would destroy me. Even though he'd been in my life for a short time, he meant more than anyone else had.

"Come back to me, Riles." He cupped my cheek and feathered his lips against mine. "No one will ever hurt you again, and I will track down every single one who has—starting with that prick Alpha, Jacob. Then the dean."

"No, please." I didn't want him at war with Jacob. The pack was fierce, and Dean Sandusky wasn't worth worrying about. "I don't want to look back when you've given me life."

And he had. I had plans, friends. *A real pack.* Things to do and a reason to be. More importantly, I was learning me. I snuggled into his warmth and sighed. "You spoil me."

"That's the plan."

He made no comment about Jacob. I knew asking an Alpha to turn away from protecting his mate was impossible. Mate. This beautiful, gorgeous man was mine. I swallowed as the emotion overpowered me. "Make love to me, Macen."

He grinned and settled his hand at my hip. "Now, that's a plan."

~A Letter From Cara Carnes~

I was thrilled to have the opportunity to write this ROAR story.

Riletta's journey from the awkward, unwanted and isolated shifter who couldn't shift to the beautiful, loved creature she was all along was a pleasure to write. I think many of us can find a piece of ourselves in her.

I must admit I have a special place in my heart for growly, alpha males who can't help but protect his mate with everything they have. Macen's harried life and need to juggle his personal desires with duty is a war I think we have all waged at one point or another.

I look forward to hearing what you think about Riletta and Macen.

cara@caracarnes.com

Book 4 in the ROAR Series
Imperfect Mate by Lia Davis

Chapter One

Where the hell did it go?

Samira frantically searched the room, tearing clothes from her dresser drawers and ripping the mound of shoes from the bottom her closet, but couldn't find the damned tablet. She swore she brought it to her room after sentinel training the night before. "Mom."

A moment later, her mother's soft, powder-like rose scent enveloped her, soothing some of the panic. Her mother had a way of calming her by just entering the room. Sam sighed as the tablet appeared in her line of sight, enclosed in its pink leather case. Taking it from her mother's grasp, Sam hugged her tight. "Thanks."

"It was where you left it." Her mother pulled back and cupped her face, forehead creasing like it did when she worried. The anxiety drifted off her, mingled with Sam's empathy, and increased her state of nervousness about leaving home. "Are you sure you're okay? I mean it's so far away."

Sam's heart warmed even though her tiger within growled in annoyance. Some would think at nineteen, she would have learned how to balance her human side with her tiger. It wasn't like she didn't know how to rein in the animal. Sam liked to let the cat rise to the surface. It gave her the edge she needed to be a good soldier. A sense of power she alone controlled. "Yes, Mom. We've talked about this. I need to do this. Dev's been going to Harmony U for four years and is now working on his master's. The independence will be good for me. And it's only a five-hour drive."

Her mother, Mary Anderson, was an older, wiser version of Sam with the same straight, thick blonde hair and ice-blue eyes. Unlike her mother, Sam was a dominant female with more energy and aggression than most of the males in the pride. She got her dominant nature from her father's alpha bloodline.

"That's five hours too far."

Sam groaned, pulled out of her mother's arms, and shoved her tablet inside her tote bag. She, as well as others in the den, didn't need to leave the pride to get degrees. Sam already had her AA in Chemistry through online classes, but she wanted the experience of working next to humans, learning their world. "Mom. I'm in more danger staying here and going through Dev's brutal sentinel training."

Sentinels were above the enforcers—soldiers who enforced pride laws—and served as the personal guards of the alpha and his family. Sam would be the first female and the youngest sentinel in the history of the Jasper Springs pride—a duty she didn't take lightly. She welcomed everything Devon threw at her.

"Not true, dear. Devon would rather cut his own head off than let anything happen to you."

Sam laughed as she led her mother down the hall to the

living room. She had a point. Dev might be her cousin, but he loved her like a little sister. He was her mentor and trainer. He was also one of her best friends.

Even though she wasn't leaving until the next morning, Sam wanted to be prepared when Dev arrived bright and early. Another reason why she'd packed days before.

Stopping in the middle of the living room, she scanned the area. Her bags and a single box sat beside the door. That was all she was taking to the university with her. Not that she wasn't allowed to bring a lot of stuff, she simply didn't have a need for too many things. Plus Dev had said the dorm rooms were smaller than her bedroom, so she'd decided to pack light.

Over the gray stone fireplace hung a family portrait. Her sixteen-year-old self sat on a high stool and her parents stood behind her, their hands rested on her shoulders. It was a little outdated, and they'd have to take another picture soon. Right after her sister arrived in a month.

Glancing over, Sam froze and her heart seemed to stop for a second. Bent at the waist, her very pregnant mother started to lift the suitcase as if to move it. She would give Sam a heart attack one day. "Mom. Put that down. It's fine where it is. Besides, Dev will get it in the morning. Didn't Asia put you on bed rest?"

The stubborn woman always insisted on doing things for herself.

"Samira, don't be silly. I feel great."

"Listen to your daughter, Mary."

The deep voice from the doorway sent a jolt of excitement through her. Spinning, she spied her father entering the small foyer. A burst of giddiness lit her inside. His brown hair was tousled like he'd fallen asleep on the flight, or maybe the car ride from the airport. Maybe both.

"Dad, you made it!" She rushed over, threw her arms around him, and squeezed.

He chuckled and wrapped his arms around her. "I

wouldn't have missed your last day home for anything."

The anxiety had built up since the day before when he hadn't shown and made her edgier the closer it got to the time Dev would drive her to Harmony Springs. She considered not going until her father showed. Yes, it was a little childish, but she didn't care. This was her first time ever leaving the pride. She needed both her parents there to see her go.

Connor Anderson was the pride's beta and sometimes assisted his twin brother, Colt, with pride business, such as acting like the alpha when it came to the council. Which was where her father had been for the past week.

"How was your trip?"

"Draining. I hate flying." He released Sam and strode over to his mate. With a swift movement, he lifted her in his arms and bit her ear. Sam blushed and looked away from her parents' playful display of affection. Their love for one another made her heart swell. They were totally devoted. They could even finish each other's sentences. It was annoying sometimes.

Following them to the sofa, she smiled wide. "You two enjoy each other, but not too much. There are still things I don't want to see." Her dad waggled his eyebrows, making Sam crinkle her nose up at them. "I'm going to fix dinner. You two behave."

Sam sighed. She hoped one day she would find a mate she could be that in love with.

03

"You nervous, kitten?"

Samira let out a low, playful growl at her cousin's question. He knew the right buttons to push her impulsive nature. Taking a deep breath, she watched out the car window as he drove through the university campus toward the dorms on the south end. Harmony University wasn't a large school, but she wouldn't describe it as small either. It was about four city blocks with three main academic buildings, several smaller buildings in between, and groups of dorms that were either apartments or houses randomly placed throughout the campus.

"I don't get nervous."

"Of course. I meant, are you excited?"

Seriously? "Why do you have to be so irritating?"

A deep chuckle rumbled through the car. "You know you love me."

"Not today." She bit her bottom lip to hide her smile.

Nervous was an understatement. She was terrified. Mixed feelings on whether she should leave home played over and over in her mind the past few months. She'd established a solid position as a junior soldier, working her way up to a sentinel. Yet, a part of her felt guilty for leaving.

Everything will be fine. Stop being a baby.

Devon pulled into a parking lot next to a large three-story brick house. Sam exited the car, mesmerized by the simple, yet beautiful home. It was not at all what she pictured for a dorm. Black shutters accented the windows against the two-tone red brick. A wide porch ran the length of the front of the house with white railing that matched the columns at each end.

After opening the back door, she removed her large, pink duffel bag and matching cosmetic case. With a bump of her hip, she closed the door and headed toward the house. She climbed the steps to the porch and waited for Dev to get the box from the truck. A swing hung at one end and a few tables and chairs scattered about the rest of the open area.

"Nice place," Dev said when he stopped next to her.

Nodding, she inhaled and sighed. "The forest is near and a stream."

Tigers, especially Samira, loved water. She could swim

all day without tiring. Dev nudged her arm and opened the door. "The dorm mother is a wolf."

Sam froze, staring at the back of her cousin's head as he entered he dorm. A wolf? It wasn't just a rumor that cats and dogs didn't get along. Well, in most cases they didn't. Sam hadn't had any experience with wolves, so she didn't know how her tiger would react to the other female.

"Are you sure? I mean…well, you know. I'm not…."

"Diversity is what your too-aggressive tiger needs to learn balance." He glanced at her over his shoulder, one brow raised in challenge. "Scared?"

She stuck her tongue out and pushed past him to enter the house. He let out a playful growl as he followed her inside. A laugh escaped her before she could rein it back in. "No." Lowering her voice, she asked, "How many humans live here?"

"Three, when the dorm is full."

Turning toward the voice, Sam found herself staring at a very dominant she-wolf. She was shorter by at least three inches than Sam. Her long, curly, black hair hung loose around her shoulders, framing her thin, yet beautiful, face. To Sam's surprise, her tiger didn't lash out or hiss at the wolf. Instead, the cat cocked her head in curiosity.

Dev, however, growled beside her, drawing Sam's attention away from the female. Raw annoyance with a hint of something else she didn't know how to describe surrounded him before he reined in his emotions, blocking Sam from getting a clear read on them. She was about to ask him what his deal was, but he spoke first. "I was told there were no other dominants in the dorm."

Ignoring Dev, the female fixed her attention on Sam and extended her hand. Nothing in the female's expression betrayed her thoughts or feelings. Her aura seemed equally quiet, not registering any reaction with Sam's empathy. *Intriguing.* "I'm Camile, a second-year student, and until they find a replacement, the acting dorm mother. I put you on the third floor with Jesse and me. I stay in the west corner. Jesse, a submissive leopard, is in the middle. You're at the other end, near the stairs."

Next to her, Dev fisted his hands and allowed his mental walls to fracture. Clearly, this female affected her cousin. Sam smiled, her earlier anxiety eased, and decided she liked Camile. Anyone who could put her cousin in his place while putting him on edge at the same time was okay by her. "That's great." Glancing at Dev, she crinkled her nose at him. "Isn't that great?"

He growled again and leaned into her. "You're a brat."

She patted his face. "I know."

Giving her attention back to Camile, Sam noticed the female's lips twitch right before she turned away to lead them up the stairs. "Only you and Jesse have arrived so far. You have a little time to familiarize yourself with the house before the others get here.

"There are three rooms and one common area on each of the second and third floors. We do sometimes eat meals together, but it's not mandatory. Some will take their meals to their rooms. This is an all-girl dorm, so no boys are allowed to sleep over."

Sam bobbed her head as she followed Camile up to the third floor. Once at the top, Camile moved to the room in the middle and gave a light tap. A moment later a small, shy female opened the door. Her brown hair was braided into two pigtails, and she had the most beautiful blue-violet eyes.

Camile offered her a warm smile. "Jesse, this is Samira. Oh, and her cousin, Devon."

The annoyance in Camile's tone as she said the latter made Sam glance behind her at Dev. He lifted one shoulder but said nothing as he slammed down his shields. No more reading his emotions for her. *Figures*. He knew her well enough she used her gift to her advantage any time she could. Sam would discover what all the tension was about between Dev and Camile one way or another. *Later, though.*

Extending her hand, Sam smiled at Jesse. The female immediately broke the brief eye contact as a spike of nervous fear rose within her, but it quickly eased before she shook Sam's hand.

"Hi. Would you like to show me around campus after I get settled?"

Jesse glanced at her, their gazes connecting briefly. A shy smile formed as warmth surrounded both of them. "I'd like that."

Sam's tiger purred, happy with the small thread of friendship springing up between them. She gave a short wave and followed Camile to the room where she'd be staying. Once inside, she glanced at Dev, who stared at her with a one-sided grin. "What?"

"I'm proud of you."

Sam rolled her eyes and tilted her head in the direction of the desk in the corner of the room as she set her bags on the bed. "Set the box over there."

Camile spoke from the doorway. "It was a gracious thing you did. Jesse is so timid and shy. This is her second year here, and she still hasn't made many friends."

Sam nodded. "She's a submissive and needs to feel needed. Her timidity is due to not knowing others."

"Yes, but you picked up on it right away."

Dev cleared his throat. "Sam is empathic. She can pick up on things others miss." He stepped closer to her, touched her cheek, and said, "I need to go check into my dorm. You okay?"

She gave him a one-arm hug. "Of course I am. Jesse and I are going sightseeing on campus."

www.ingramcontent.com/pod-product-compliance
Lightning Source LLC
Chambersburg PA
CBHW060432130626
46555CB00005B/2315